Calling Extra

KRISTINA ROMERO

ISBN-13: 978-0-9851916-0-3
ISBN-10: 0985191600

Library of Congress Control Number: 2012902913

Book Website
www.callingextra.com
Email: info@callingextra.com

Give feedback on the book at:
feedback@callingextra.com

First Edition

For my loving and supportive parents,
and Daniel, my real life Grin.

CONTENTS

"The golden moments in the stream of life rush past us, and we see nothing but sand. The angels come to visit us, and we only know them when they are gone. How shall we live so as at the end to have done the most for others and make the most of ourselves?"

- George Eliot

CHAPTER I

July 15, 1899

The last day of my youth began with the shatter of a plate and the piercing scream of an infant. I awoke in my small tenement before the sun had barely stirred. The air filtered in through cracks in the wall and was bitter cold, but the upcoming hot summer day would change that soon enough.

It was Friday, and my father was already roused and dressing for work. He glanced down at me with a smile. "*Guten Morgen.*"

"Good morning," I mumbled back in English.

"Now, up," he said sharply.

I exhaled, bit my lip, and pulled back the covers, exposing myself to the frigid air. I slipped on my rubber-soled boots, a gift from my mother before she died. She once told me they represented equality and would lead me places beyond my wildest dreams, but all they did was constantly break apart at the seams, forcing me to wrap the laces around the bottom to keep the soles on my feet. I often searched for ways to slip them off. Maybe my bare feet didn't represent equality, but they felt freer than being bound in broken shoes.

"Keep them on today," my father stressed. *"Muss immer getragen werden."*

Every day my father felt he needed to remind me to keep my boots on "at all times." But I knew at thirteen that my father wasn't truly giving reminders—he was giving instructions.

As usual, deafening screams interrupted us. Our tenement was always filled with the noises and smells of Mrs. Krol, the Polish widow with whom we boarded, and her five children. The bitter woman often lingered close to our half of the room, bouncing her wailing child on her hip to calm him.

Mrs. Krol frequently pleaded for me to take the screaming boy in my bed since there was no room in hers. She sometimes bribed me with a Liberty Head nickel, but I would decline. No amount of money was worth having such shrieks so close to my ear.

That morning I didn't have a job waiting for me. The day before, the Joseph Luby tailor shop suffered a terrible fire, nearly killing three workers. This was the first day since my mother's death that I was not spending at the shop.

I leaned forward behind the calico sheet that divided our small tenement so that I didn't have to see Mrs. Krol struggling through her morning routine. "I knew it was going to happen," I said softly.

"*Was*, Elsie?" Papa asked in German, slicing a stiff loaf of bread for our breakfast.

"I knew the fire was going to happen. There were always spare scraps on the floor near the gaslights. There was only one exit for the girls and one small bucket of water. I should have said something."

Papa kneeled down and took my hands in his. "It's not your place to get involved in such matters. You would have been let go for saying such things. There will always be someone else for that. You stay quiet and keep to yourself. It's the only way to keep your job."

I always believed what Papa said, but there was something inside of me that knew my silence in that instance had been wrong.

"*Ja?*"

"Yes…" I nodded in agreement.

"Good, so you come with me to the railroad today. There are flower girls who work outside Vanderbilt. You will ask them where you can do the same. But keep those boots on!" he scolded.

The sun was now peeking over the tenement across the street, and the warmth was creeping across the laundry line toward our window.

"Come." He lifted me up off the bed and nestled me into his six-foot frame. He was my protector and all I had.

"Dietrich, if the child is not going to work today, she should stay here and help with the small ones," Mrs. Krol demanded.

I cowered. Her stare was sharper than my father's razor. "We pay to board," my father said. "Unless you desire to pay her for her time?"

Mrs. Krol scoffed. She would never pay me. Too often she treated me like a child. I was thirteen, but because of my small frame I still looked ten, so people often treated me like a child.

"Well, that settles it." Papa winked as he whisked me out the door.

In the dark hallway of the tenement, I stepped over two young street traders curled up along the wall. They were no more than eight years old and reeked of sewers and spoiled milk. I tried to cough out the smell. I wasn't sure if the stench came from the two boys or if it was the normal smell of the hallways. In our tenement, most of the time it was hard to determine where unpleasant aromas came from.

"They shouldn't be sleeping here," I mumbled to my father.

"Elsie, quiet," Papa scolded.

Papa was right. I knew I had no place to look down on them, but I hated their crass voices and the freedom they flaunted. We paid four dollars a month for our half room shared with Mrs. Krol. These boys paid nothing and still received suitable shelter in our hallway.

In fact, as we approached Vanderbilt and 42nd, a similar newsboy was yelling on the street corner, crowing on about his wares. "Man found dead by railroad. Crushed skull! Killer on the loose!"

I sped up to escape the shrill of his call, but the front lip of my rubber sole caught on the pavement and bent backwards, sending me diving to the ground. Immediately a hand scooped me upright.

"Thank you, Papa." I brushed myself off. Yet when I looked up, it was not Papa's face that peered down at me but the shouting newsboy's wide, toothy grin.

"Ya all right, lady?"

"Fine."

He let out a light laugh. It was carefree. I clenched my teeth, reminding myself to be polite, and forced a smile as I scurried to join my father a few paces ahead.

Curious, I looked back at the boy who had already returned to hawking the daily paper. I noticed he wasn't a boy at all. Nearly fifteen, he was tall with messy brown hair tucked under his cap. His face had soft features, but his wide smile wrinkled at the corners with a simple right dimple. It held the most weight on his face, drawing an admirer right to it. No dirt had collected around his brow like the other newsboys, but it was still early in the day. Most unusual, though, was a book tucked neatly in the rear of his trousers between his pants and the small of his back.

Suddenly, he peeked over his shoulder and caught my stare. I flinched. But just as I was about to turn away, he offered me one more wide, sly grin.

Papa was right about the flower girls at 42nd and Vanderbilt: there were a lot, too many, in fact. I was nervous as we approached.

"Maybe I can just come inside with you first? I've always wanted to see where you work," I offered up to Papa.

Papa let out a breath. Work had not been easy for him since the freight handlers and surface railroad men of New Jersey and Brooklyn had gone on strike. Many of the disgruntled men had migrated to Manhattan to work in the train yards, jeopardizing my father's employment.

"Just a few minutes. But keep silent like a good girl."

Once inside the train shed at 42nd, I immediately felt the cool relief from the hot sun that had already burned up the frigid morning air.

The bottom of my sole flipped under my boot again. Frustrated, I kicked the pair off and placed my bare feet along the cold steel of the railway. I held my shoes close to my side, ready to slip them back on if Papa noticed. I glanced up at my father, but his eyes weren't on me; they were focused ahead intently.

"What's wrong?"

Papa's brow lowered. I followed as he walked ahead. His gaze was fixed on a horde of men that had gathered at the center of one of the tracks. When the group saw the six-foot figure of my father, they turned and headed for him. As they moved closer, three constables mixed among them drifted to the front of the mob.

A scrawny man cowered behind them, hands clutched around his cap like he was wringing water from its corners. He lifted a shaky finger and pointed it in our direction. The shortest constable followed the accusing gesture and walked our way with a tense fervor.

"What is your name?" stated the man.

"Dietrich Lutz," my father mumbled, confused.

The worker nodded. "That is he. That is the German."

The constable seized my father by the shoulder. Papa was speechless.

"What are you doing, let go of him!" I shouted.

I ran after the crowd as it forced him outside into the bright sun. His fellow workers were mumbling words like "immigrant" and "anarchist." I made out something that sounded like "killed."

Fighting through the mass, I surfaced only in time to see uniformed men place my father in a police wagon. The back door of bars swung closed, and he clutched them with his hands, a criminal.

They asked no questions, and never bothered to give explanations. I could tell that my father's silence was frustrating him. He didn't have the English words to argue, and I could see his brain working to figure out the reason for his abduction. He was confused, his brow furrowed the way it was when he couldn't solve the problem that plagued our cast-iron stove.

"Elsie!" he shouted as the wagon took off. "*Sie gehen nach...*" He searched for the word in English. "Home...*warte auf mich.*" But I couldn't go home, even though he insisted.

Horror filled me as I realized that my father was being taken from me. I ran after him, clutching my boots in my hand, now regretting I had taken them off. The faster I ran, the sharper the pain.

Tears streamed down my faced. "Help me! Someone help me!"

The jagged gravel ripped through the bottoms of my feet. There was no way I could catch him, and even if I did, it meant nothing. But I ran anyway, the dips, holes, and sewage of 42nd Street fighting against me.

It wasn't long until the wagon was completely out of sight. Defeated, I began to sob. A woman grabbed my shoulder.

"Dear, settle yourself." Her voice was sweet and rang like a church bell. She peered down at my feet, so dirty now that they blended right in with the street.

"Young lady, put on your shoes!"

"Papa, they've taken Papa!" was all I could say.

"The constable?"

"Yes, I need to help him!" I shouted.

"Where is your mother?"

"She died. He is all I have. Can you take me to him?" Pleading, I buried my face in her soft black velvet shoulder. She didn't mind and clutched me closer, trying to soothe my sobs with gentle hushes.

"It will be all right, dear."

After a quick second, she released me. Taking my face with her hand, she lifted my chin.

"He is all you have, no mother?" she asked.

"No…" I stopped. The moment the words escaped my mouth, I knew. A chill ran down my spine, and I finally looked into the face of the unknown woman. The gentle and caring face belonged to a Reformer, a woman dedicated to cleaning the streets of the city from orphans and runaways.

"Come with me." Her voice was no longer sweet but stern, like the turn a friendly manager takes when he senses the boss is near. It was all business.

"Put your shoes on."

Ashamed, I slipped my shoes on my tender and injured feet. I felt like a fool, a child whose emotions had got the best of her. I tried to call to mind a way to fix my mistake. I wanted to run to Mrs. Krol, but I knew she wouldn't care for me.

Reluctantly, I followed the woman as she led me to a nearby gray stone building. I walked solemnly, swearing off emotions forever, my heart torn out and left for the street cleaners on the corner of 42nd and 5th.

CHAPTER II

Asylum

I had never noticed, nor cared to, the Orphan Asylum for Young Girls on East 44th Street. It was a plain, stoned-faced, five-story building with rows of ten windows dotted like Morse code across each floor.

The Reformer released my wrist and sat me in a chair outside a small office. In the dim light of the hallway, I could see that she was in her thirties, tall and lanky with long fingers that did not display a wedding band. Her name was Miss Sophia Dannon, and she worked for the Society for Public Charity and Relief of Destitute Children. A profession, it appeared, she enjoyed.

She left me in the hall and entered the superintendent's office to speak fervently with the elderly man behind the desk. I sat quietly, watching through the windowpane on the door as the Reformer gave her reasons for "saving me."

"Robert," the Reformer began, "she has nothing, and I am certain she has not been schooled."

"Not been schooled? At thirteen?" He sounded surprised.

"I have sent someone from the Society to check on her father and have him sign over her care to this orphanage. If not, it is nothing for a county magistrate or law authority to get an official ruling."

"We are short a matron due to Helen's sudden affliction…" He nodded, thinking.

The lady smiled, pleased to have fulfilled his need. "I am sure it will be no problem for the girl to watch the younger ones, at least until you replace Helen. The girl seems respectable. It appears that the mother instilled good morals in the child before she passed."

As she spoke, I recalled how places like this would often send older children away and indenture them to work for a family. However, I knew staying in the asylum could be worse.

"Come Elisabeth," Miss Dannon demanded as she left the office.

"My name is Elsie," I responded, following her down a long hall.

"No dear, it is Elisabeth. A respectable girl does not have a nickname."

"But it's not a nick—"

"They have two hundred girls here. Short uncommon names are too much for the matrons to remember."

We stopped at a room at the end of a long hallway. It was similar to a small hospital room, with a stripped bed, white walls, and metal basin. Standing there waiting was a nurse fingering a clipboard.

"Strip down to your undergarments," she said.

While inspecting me, she asked questions about scarlet fever, influenza, whooping cough, and other illnesses. The nurse was quite disturbed by my admission that my mother had died of typhoid fever and gave a sharp look at the Reformer. Miss Dannon was quick to chime in.

"How long ago did your mother pass?" Miss Dannon asked in a singsong tone.

"Three years," I mumbled.

The nurse nodded approvingly. She continued to fill out her checklist with my name, which somehow became Elisabeth, my birthdate, my former place of residence (43 Orchard Street), my physical condition (healthy), and that I had been vaccinated (about which she never asked).

"We rarely take on girls older than twelve," she sneered. "You will need to work very hard and help the matrons with the small children."

The nurse handed me a secondhand uniform that was extremely small and uncomfortable. She then turned to Miss Dannon. "The child is healthy. There shouldn't be any problem."

The Reformer gave one nod and headed for the door.

"Wait, miss, what about...?" I stumbled to my feet, wanting to know more about want she intended to do about my father.

The lady stopped, turned swiftly, and gave a knowing smile. "You will be good here," she stated matter-of-factly. "I will see to it that your father sends a letter."

She gave one more nod to the nurse, then her black velvet figure whisked out the door. I was surprised that for all her insistence and bullying to place me in the institution, she could leave without a kind word.

Matron O'Donnell was a strong, stout woman with a fierce hand. She showed me to my bed by simply pointing to it from the other end of the long room that housed one hundred cots.

"Third from the window."

She turned on her heels and expected me to follow immediately. When I paused, she shot me a look of disgust, "Young lady, this is a place of virtue and morals. You will be expected to listen to your matrons, your teachers, and all authoritative figures."

I nodded quickly and didn't waste a second to join her at her side as she moved to the next room.

"We will send someone over to your previous place of residence to recover your belongings. However, we lead a simple Christian life here at the asylum, so anything that acts as a distraction will be forbidden."

I knew not to expect the arrival of any of my possessions. Mrs. Krol would hide any that were of worth the minute she discovered my father and I would not be returning.

Down the hall, we arrived at a classroom where the girls were in the midst of reading and writing with their McGuffey Readers.

"We school all year round," the matron said to my disappointment. "Idle hands are the devil's workshop."

The Reformer had been right in her assumption. I had not been schooled, at least of late. My father needed me to work a full day. It was the only way for both of us to survive.

My palms sweated as the matron silenced the teacher with her mere appearance.

"Sit," I was instructed.

The last time I had been in a schoolroom was the year before my mother passed. I couldn't recall anything I had learned. As the instruction continued, I kept my head down, closed my eyes, and continually prayed not to be called upon.

After three hours of schooling, I followed the sea of girls into the dining hall. My spirits were briefly lifted at the joyous sight of boiled meat, potatoes, mutton broth, and fruit. As the scent of food whiffed through my nose, I could barely wait for the finish of the prayer before devouring the lot.

I shoved the food into my mouth quickly, but by my second scoop, a hand came down quickly, knocking the boiled meat from my spoon and sending it rolling down the table.

"Young lady, please mind your manners. As an older girl, you are an example," the fair-skinned matron known as Miss Booth declared. She casually moved on to the next table after her scolding. I stared at the fallen meat, tempted to pick it up but wary of the punishment that might follow.

The dining hall quickly filled with a symphony of spoons clinking on soup bowls. As I tried to settle the hunger pains in my stomach, I noticed various faces staring at me through their slurps. Most ranged in the ages of five to eight. There were a few that looked a year or two younger than me. One small face of an Irish girl caught my eye. I smiled, but she diverted her stare quickly back down to her plate. It was clear that these girls were not in the habit of making new friends.

Before I could finish my soup, Matron O'Donnell grasped my shoulder. She signaled for me to collect the plates. Timid, I rose and followed her lead, but not without tucking an orange into my pocket for later.

Two other girls joined me. One was scrawny and short with matted, curly hair, and the other was thicker with a large nose and beady eyes. As I washed the dishes, the two whispered in each other's ear, giggling.

"Come on, the faster you finish, the sooner we can play potsies," the littler one said.

"Sorry," I mumbled and continued with the dishes.

Suddenly a crash sent me stumbling back, fractures of a white plate falling to my feet. I whipped around to look at the stout girl next to me, smiling smugly.

"Did you drop that plate?" screamed the matron from the other side of the kitchen. She stormed over to me.

I glanced down at the broken plate, confused. The scrawny girl chuckled underneath her breath.

"It wasn't me," I stuttered.

15

"Rebecca and Josephine have been washing dishes here for two years."

"Well…" I began, "I didn't even touch it."

"I saw her," interjected the troublemaker, the heavy girl with beady eyes.

"Hand me the fruit in your pocket," demanded the matron.

I slowly dipped into the front pocket of the undersized uniform and pulled out the orange, handing it over reluctantly.

"You will surrender your breakfast privileges for tomorrow. We do not have extra plates for you to break as you will." The matron stomped out, clutching the only surviving piece of my dinner at her side

"Why did you do that?" I chastised.

"You better know the rules," the stout girl hissed back.

"But you were the one that broke the plate."

"No, our rules, not theirs!" the scrawny girl added.

"We are in charge. We run this place, and you better answer to us."

I was too angry to speak. They were younger than I was, and at least the same height. I knew I could show them a lesson, but that was foolish. I had never been taught to fight, never had a reason to. Instead, I swallowed my anger, finished all the dishes in silence, and then left the kitchen.

After a series of prayers, we were sternly instructed for bedtime at eight thirty. Summer rain poured down from the skies and tapped on the windows. I was told to assist the young children in getting undressed and to help them into their beds.

When nine o'clock came, the lights were blown out and the noises began. Continuous coughs, muffled crying, and giggling from the older girls mixed in with the rain. I was somewhat pleased at all the noise. Silence would have only allowed for reflection, how I hated this place and how I was disgusted at how much my life had changed in an instant. I was determined to find out what had happened to my father and restore our humble life, even if it meant escaping a dry bed that rested safely behind stone walls.

CHAPTER III

Grin

The next morning before arithmetic, Matron O'Donnell informed me that my father had sent a letter and had consented to my stay, promising he would pay the asylum for past dues when he was released. I knew Papa's promise to pay them wasn't true. I figured they would eventually indenture me to a family for their money.

"Where is the letter?" I asked.

"It was a letter to the superintendent, dear," she said, walking off.

Fire burned inside me. I had to see that letter.

"They keep the letters in a file," whispered Emma, the small Irish girl from the night before. "The only way you see them is when you're sick."

"And you never read them?" I asked.

"One time I was sick with fever and they showed me a letter from my mum. I guess they thought it would help lift my spirits."

"What'd she say?"

"She hoped I would get better and she would come get me soon." Emma tried to hide her disappointment that this had yet to happen.

"I need to know what my father said, and it'll be hard to fake a fever," I said under my breath.

The teacher entered the room, and the girls were silenced. My mind drifted during the lesson. There was only one time I could get into that office, during the hours the girls left for work outside the asylum.

After lunch, I devised my plan. As long as I appeared to be working, I knew that the matrons would not pay me any attention. I took the mop and the bucket from the end of the hall outside the bedroom and walked down the stairs to the lower floor.

I quietly mopped closer and closer to the superintendent's office, my heart beating faster with every step. As I brushed the mop under the door, it opened and a plump gray-haired man stepped out.

"Excuse me, sir," I said quickly.

To my relief, he merely grunted and stepped over the pooled water, letting the door close behind him. Quickly I slid the bar of soap between the door and the wall to prop it open.

Emma appeared. "There you are."

"I need you to watch the door, make sure no one comes in."

She didn't respond, but I didn't have time to negotiate with her.

"Tap the door if you hear anyone."

She gave a reluctant nod, and in an instant I pried open the door, removed the soap, and slid inside.

The file cabinet was in the corner, and I moved to it quickly. Shifting through, I found my file, "Elizabeth Lutz." There was the one page from the nurse and then a single letter with only a couple handwritten lines.

Dear Sur:
i am the man who child is in you plase. i wish to no she is well and that she lurns good. let her no this. thak you vearry kindly
Dietrich Lutz

My heart sank. It was his handwriting and barely legible. There was no envelope with an address or any trace of where it had come from.

Suddenly, the door opened, revealing the superintendent, his face flushed red with anger. Matron O'Donnell stood beside him, with Emma hiding behind her. The fierce woman swiftly grabbed my wrist and removed me from the office so quickly that I couldn't keep up with the punishment she shouted.

Emma's eyes were dry and unapologetic. She had turned me in. My anger boiled over from her betrayal, but I stayed silent. Papa had told me that I couldn't trust anyone, and at that moment I understood what he meant. Without hesitation, the matron backhanded me across the face and abandoned me in a broom closet that she locked from the outside.

After a short period of isolation "in order to incite reflection," I was put to work. The scrubbing of the pine boards didn't change their color or the stains that had scarred them for so many years. All it did was change the feeling in my arm, which sped up whenever Matron O'Donnell walked by the room. I never minded hard labor, but I did mind free labor, and the asylum was exhausting me of all I could give.

I remembered watching my mother scrub the floors of our tenement. She would painstakingly scrub each board with a tireless effort, sometimes humming and even smiling. She did everything with passion and intensity, even menial tasks. It was something I felt I didn't inherit. My father was more subdued and quiet, taking in the world around him. Even my mother had remarked that I was like my father, which is why memories of her seemed like mysteries I never got the chance to solve.

"Breakout!" rang a voice from an open window. It clearly distinguished itself from the clopping of the horses and squeaking of the wagons with a bold roar. "Policeman shot dead in a breakout!"

I rushed to the second-story window and leaned over. Only one floor below me was the loud newsboy. I immediately noticed the book tucked in the back of his trousers held up by red suspenders. When he turned, sensing an onlooker, I instantly recognized his smile.

He tipped his hat and then continued on with his wares, apparently not recognizing me.

"Pardon me? Boy!" I called down.

"Yes, miss."

I half expected him to offer me his paper, but he didn't.

"Is that breakout a real story?"

He looked over his shoulder and came closer to the window.

"Why do ya wanna know?"

I didn't know what to say. I didn't want to trust him.

"Think it's someone ya know?" he chuckled.

"Is it real or not?" I shot back.

His voice dropped down to a whisper. "Nah, made it up."

I didn't know whether to feel relieved or not.

"What's he in for?"

I paused, not wanting to release any information.

"Hey, I told ya the story was fake." He grinned.

"It's my father, and I don't know," I said. "He was taken away last week, and I was put here before I could figure anything out."

"I remember ya now." He dropped his papers to his side. "I saw that. Ya and your pa, outside the train station."

My heart raced. "Did you see where they took him?"

"I know where they would 'ave."

"Could you find out for me? I'll pay you!"

"With what?" he laughed.

"I'll find something," I stated back firmly.

"Is he all ya got?"

My eyes drifted low. I didn't want him to see them filling up with tears.

"I know all about lonely, orphan girl," he said calmly. "I'll find your pa for ya."

My heart leapt. I tried to hide my excitement with a simple smile.

"Ya just find a way to be in the alley after the sun sets. I should be back with news by then."

"You really think you can find out where he is?"

"Soytenly. I'm a newsie."

I didn't know if I could trust him, not after Emma so easily turned me in. But he had no reason to tell the matrons, and if he didn't come back at all, that wasn't too bad either.

"Dietrich Lutz," I finally informed him.

"What's *ya* name?" he said without missing a beat.

I paused then gave in. "Elsie."

He tipped his hat again and added, "I'm Grin. Nice to meet ya."

Before I could say anything else, Grin was gone in a flash back toward Midtown.

I spent the rest of the day thinking of Grin. I wondered what his real name was, where he had come from, and if he was like the newsboys I had seen sleeping in the hall of my tenement. I was curious to know why there was a book tucked in his trousers and if he always smiled at everyone the way he smiled at me. Then, realizing my vanity had got the best of me, I tried hard to force my mind onto a different subject.

The latter part of the day was spent atoning for my sins in chapel and in quiet prayer. The silence of the asylum was deafening. I had lived with work, noise, and constant chaos my whole life. It helped me not to dwell upon the sensitive subjects of my heart. But now I had nothing but time to think, and in the stillness I was reminded again of my mother.

She and Papa had loved each other very much and had lived through the death of two children, who would have been my older sisters. She never wanted me to work. It was only after she died that I left school to do work. In fact, it was my mother's position at the Joseph Luby tailor shop that I replaced. Before she died, she tried to teach me everything she knew, and she had hoped school would fill in the rest. She had big dreams for me.

The month my mother died, she developed a cough and complained of a headache. She refused to let it slow her, insisting that she continue work at the shop. But by the second week, my mother was bedridden with a high fever. She became increasingly nervous and would only speak in German. When flat, rose-colored spots appeared on her chest, Papa and I knew that she had been stricken with typhoid fever. By the third week, her mind was gone.

One night, she called me by name to her bedside. "Elsie," she stuttered out. I rushed to her side. For her to refer to me by name was rare. She hadn't called either one of us by name for days by that time.

"Yes, Mama," I replied.

"You must speak up," she said in German, her eyes not focused on me but turned out toward the sky.

"I'm right here," I said louder in her ear.

She turned and looked me in the eyes, grabbing my hand with a smile. "Speak up. You have a strong voice."

I looked at Papa, who just shook his head, attributing her wayward comments to delirium.

My papa had hoped she would make it through, heard of many who had, but come the end of the month, she passed late in the night.

The bell rang, signaling time for supper. My mind turned to the thought of reuniting with Grin and hearing news of my papa. Just like the night before, one of the matrons gave me a job in the kitchen. I hoped that it was to remove the meat from the cellar and I could steal some for Grin as payment. But all she did was gesture to a box of spoiled potatoes in my path and advised me to take them outside to the trash.

Once in the alley, the warm humid New York air filled my lungs. I tried not to breathe in too deep because of my proximity to the trash heap. As the time passed with no sign of Grin, I felt like a fool for trusting a stranger. Then a voice came out of the darkness.

"He's at the Tombs on Centre."

I was so surprised at his appearance that I spilled the rotten potatoes to the ground. Luckily, I didn't have to gather them since the rats attacked them immediately.

"You found him?"

"Sure did, not too many respondin' to the name Lutz. He's a tall fella."

"That's him!" I shouted, but Grin's expression changed my enthusiasm.

"Bad news. He's in for killin'."

"Killing?"

Grin nodded and leaned against the stone wall, tucking his hands in his pockets. I was too stunned to move.

"Durin' an incident with the trolley strikers, they say he shot a cop," he explained.

"He didn't do it. I'm sure he wasn't there. I know him. He wouldn't."

"I believe ya, but it's not that easy for ones like us."

"What do you mean?"

"Slum folk."

"I need to get him out."

"From the Tombs?" he laughed. "Good luck."

I wanted to argue, but Grin knew more than I did.

"No need to be hopeless," he said. "There's ways of gettin' him out, and ya right, ya are gonna need money to get a top-notch lawyer."

"A lawyer?"

"Sure, it'd be easier to just bribe the cops at the Tombs, but it'd cost just as much for a lawyer, maybe more. How much do ya get here?"

"Nothing," I replied solemnly.

"You could be a newsie if ya wanna," he shrugged.

"What do you make?"

"Twenty-five cents a day when the news is respectable. During the war we'd sometimes make fifty."

"I'll need a war," I spat out without thinking.

26

Grin laughed. I couldn't help but join him despite my desperate situation. His company seemed familiar. His offer was tempting but dangerous.

"I was hoping to pay you with the spare meat, but they sent me to dump the rotten potatoes instead."

"Ah, I don't mind, it was nothin'."

"I have to get back inside," I said quickly.

"I'll be here tomorra," he stated casually. "If ya wanna talk again."

"Thank you."

He picked up a stack of papers from behind the wall. "Theaters will be gettin' out in half an hour. It's a good spot."

And with that, he walked off back down the alley, leaving me with thoughts like racehorses galloping through my head. As long as I stayed at the asylum, I wouldn't be able to help my father at all. But outside the asylum, I had no place to stay, and no factory would hire me, at least none that hired from the tenements. Maybe a life with the newsboys was my way, my only way.

Chapter IV

The Great White Way

The next day, I was awoken by a scream from the outside hall. Like the other girls, I jumped out of bed and ran to see what was the matter. The door to the hallway was already open, and a young girl was standing over the body of Matron O'Donnell, who was writhing in madness, her arms bent toward her, unable to speak. Her body jolted in spasms on the ground like she had no control of her limbs. It was a terrible sight.

The girl who had come to find her in this state was crying uncontrollably. "I'd just come out to go to the washroom, and there she was!"

A flood of matrons and the superintendent, wrapped in his morning robe, stopped in horror at the sight.

"Call the nurse!" cried one of the matrons while feeling Matron O'Donnell's pulse.

After a few hours of gossip, speculation and crude jokes, news eventually traveled through the asylum that Matron O'Donnell had recovered. The perpetrator seemed to be the medicine she had taken. Sinisterly, her cough medicine had been replaced with the sleeping medicine laudanum. Matron O'Donnell had taken the highly concentrated dose from what appeared to be her traditional bottle. Suspicion was that someone in the asylum switched the bottle. Rebecca and Josephine were nowhere in sight.

At the announcement of this rumor, many of the asylum girls crowded around the door of the superintendent's office to eavesdrop on the recovering Matron O'Donnell and her accusations. But one didn't need to be outside the door to hear Matron O'Donnell screaming at the top of her lungs.

"It was one of the children. I know it to be true!"

I decided to stay clear of the drama, but when I heard a flurry of steps ascending to my floor, I ran to the join the commotion. The crowd rushing up the stairs abruptly stopped in front of me. The superintendent folded his arms, glaring at me with accusatory eyes. I quickly realized that in such a large institution, it was easy to blame the newcomer. I was to be the scapegoat.

I was locked in the superintendent's office for an hour until Miss Booth finally entered.

"We are sending you to work for a family," said Miss Booth.

"Why?" I was able to mumble.

"You will be better there. They will care for you until you are old enough to be hired at a lucrative position. Payment, of course, will be received here at the asylum until your debt is paid."

I didn't know what to say. My voice froze up inside my throat. I swallowed hard.

"When?"

"Once we finish with the paperwork, we should be able to relocate you by morning."

I dug my heels into the floorboards. They were not going to send me off to be a slave, to work for people who could easily be worse than Mrs. Krol was. It was then I made my decision. I only needed to wait for supper to sneak out.

It was easier that I didn't have any possessions. I was right in my assumption that none would be recovered from Mrs. Krol. I didn't even have my old clothes. But what I did have was an unusual trust in Grin.

Supper was delicious. I ate as much as I could without appearing unladylike to the matrons, who would have removed my plate from me. I figured if I ate enough, it could last me a few days.

After I finished, I waited for Miss Booth to approach and give me my task in the kitchen. She did not. I started to get nervous when I saw the two devilish girls, Rebecca and Josephine, stand and move to their chores.

I immediately got up, hoping to beat them to the kitchen. Miss Booth's eyes followed me. I had made it to the pile of food crates from the cellar when the matron entered.

"Young lady," she said in a stern voice.

I took a deep breath and turned.

"There is no need for your work this evening. Please return to your table."

Rebecca and Josephine joined her side. They had, as usual, been spreading lies that I was stealing.

Her eyes fixed themselves into an unyielding glare. I questioned running for the door. There was no way she could catch me.

"I wanted to help this evening," I replied.

She raised one eyebrow in suspicion. "And why is that?"

My mind raced to find an answer. "I feel a heavy burden on my heart for what happened to Matron O'Donnell. I know that through my labor, I may be able to atone for my sin."

"Chapel and prayer," the matron added instantly.

"Yes, and chapel and silent prayer," I reiterated.

There was a moment of tense thought. Rebecca and Josephine were itching to protest.

"Indeed," she finally relented. "Remove the crates and sweep the floors before retiring." She turned to the girls. "If you see her take anything, immediately apprehend her."

I knew I had to act quickly. Lifting the crates, I spotted a tomato and an apple. With the two girls' backs turned, I snuck them under my garment and moved out the back.

Flinging the crates on the pile of trash, I waited anxiously in the eerie night. The darkness was overwhelming, and I wondered if I should start out down the alley before the matron or Rebecca and Josephine came looking for me.

My legs shivered from nerves. I hoped I could trust Grin to return to me. Otherwise, I would never be able to find him again.

The cackling laughs of Rebecca and Josephine sounded from inside. My heart raced.

That was it. I had made up my mind, and within an instant, my shivering legs were moving fast down the alley. I continued to clutch the apple and the tomato under my uniform. My fears were temporarily silenced as I focused on running as fast as I could away from the asylum.

I had no clue whether I was moving west or east, downtown or up toward Midtown. My mind was swimming with what I had just done. As I rested on the corner of a residential street, I knew there was still time to go back. I shook my head. No way would I go back. Then I remembered the theaters of Midtown. If Grin had forgotten, he would be there, ready to sell his papers to the theatergoers.

I glanced up at the street sign, 39th. Turning my body north, I took a breath and charged uptown.

The Brush arc lamps along the Great White Way near Longacre Square were a signal of freedom as I stopped on the corner of Broadway and 45th Street. The area was quiet. The theaters had not yet let out. I looked around for some newsboys, figuring they would know Grin.

A whistle echoed from behind me. I turned and

was surprised to see it was aimed at me. It was a newsboy but not Grin. He was gangly, with coarse stubble growing in on his chin. His oversized nightshirt was half-tucked into worn trousers. His hair, greasy, dripped long over his ears.

"Pape for the lady?" He licked his lips, holding up a paper. His approach made me cringe.

I decided to ignore him and not ask about Grin. But five other boys of various heights and sizes soon joined him. They moved closer. I looked around, desperate for any sign of help. The street was deserted. It appeared I was going to be their fun until it was time to work.

"Why youse out so late?" he snarled. His face edged in close to mine. His breath smelled. Then, with his eyes inches from mine, I realized the reason for his proximity.

"You gonna give me that fruit, or am I gonna 'ave to take it?"

I quickly removed the tomato and apple from my dress, ready to throw them at him and run, but at that moment a fist reached around the outside of the boy's chin and socked him good and hard. The boy fell to the ground inches from my feet. I stumbled back.

Grin shook his wrist. "Rat, ya lousy mutt, get out of here or I'll get the Vincent boys to kick your slats in."

The boy got up off the ground and stared at Grin eye to eye. "I'll get youse, Grin." He spat, signaling his boys to follow him. Grin spat on the ground as they passed by.

When all was clear, he turned to me. "Ya alright?"

I nodded.

"I see ya broke out! If I had known, I would have come to ya earlier. No need to be walkin' the streets all alone around these parts."

"So you were going to come?"

"Soytenly! I was on my way down when I saw you runnin' up here like ya five-fingered somethin'," he laughed.

"Who was that?"

"Oh, Rat…nevermind him. He's the worst kind of nothin'."

Something about the menace didn't bother Grin at all. But I sensed that this Rat boy was trouble.

"Come on," Grin continued. "I'll show ya how I work."

Warmth erupted from the opened doors of the Lyceum Theatre as the patrons rushed out into the glow of the dimly lit street. They scattered in every direction. The perfume of the women and the whiskey breath of the men filled the air along with the chatter as people discussed the play with fervor.

I waited for Grin to start, but he just leaned back and smiled at me.

"Go on!" I prodded.

"Why don't ya?" he goaded back, handing me a paper. "Ya a newsie now."

I took the paper and his challenge. I spotted a wealthy woman with a string of pearls around her neck. "That one?" I asked Grin.

"Go ahead," he said signaling that the woman was getting away.

"Miss," I said.

"Loudly!" Grin shouted back.

"Miss!" I shouted, but she barely even reacted. "Buy the *Evening Journal*?"

She shimmied by me with barely a glance. Grin shook his head in disapproval.

"Come on then!" I shot back. "You do it."

"I'm having a much better time watchin' ya," he teased.

I huffed and tried again.

"*Evening Journal*!" I waved the paper back and forth over my head.

Now Grin was doubled over in laughter. I marched back toward him. "What is so funny?"

He could barely speak. "Nothin', just…watchin' is all," he was able to mutter out.

I shoved the paper back to him. "Go ahead. Sell your wares."

"No, please, try again. But be smart. What do they wanna know?"

"I don't know."

"Ya the only one that can tell them what's in that pape," he smiled. "Have ya even looked in it?"

"You've seen me," I chided.

He opened the paper and handed it to me.

"Looks like a whole bunch of mosquitoes in Chicago, more than usual, it says." Grin seemed pleased with this. "Millions, terrifyin' the humble folk of the city!"

"Alright," I nodded, starting to get it.

I went back out into the crowd. "Extra! Millions of demonic pests swarming Chicago! The whole city in panic!"

A man in a tall black hat with a handlebar mustache swiped the paper from my hands. "Let me see that!"

"Penny, sir!" I shot back.

He dropped a penny in my hand, found the section in the paper, and glared down at me before walking away.

"I did it!" I skipped back to Grin holding up my single shiny coin. "I sold a paper."

"A *pape*," Grin corrected.

"A pape," I repeated.

"Nice work," he nodded. "Ya see, we're entertainers, and this is our play."

After my lesson, Grin set himself into motion. He went through a whole bunch of stories I didn't know were in the paper. I was honored when he also used my "mosquitoes in Chicago" story. After he had rid himself of all his "papes," he rejoined me by the side of the theater.

"It's gettin' late now." He fiddled with the change in his pocket. "We better start out."

"Where?"

"Ya wanna sleep, don't ya!" he laughed, dropping a nickel into my hand.

"What's this?"

"A nickel, your first day's pay," Grin smiled.

He headed back down Broadway, and I followed behind.

Grin led me down past Midtown, then Greenwich, and finally to the heart of downtown Manhattan. Just when I was going to ask to rest, he stopped in sight of St. Paul's Chapel with its single tall bell tower.

"Quiet," he whispered, waving his hand for me to follow him.

We crept in the gate and tiptoed past the headstones that lay at the front grounds of the church. Grin stopped at a hatch that appeared to go to a lower floor underneath the church from the outside. He unhooked the open hinge and moved into the darkness. I hesitated.

"Comin'?"

With nowhere else to go, I nodded and followed. The church was empty, but Grin continued to take care not to make any sounds. To my relief, Grin was not venturing farther down into the ground but around a corner that led to a stairway upward.

We went up the stairs until we reached another hatch, this opening to an attic. I climbed in just as Grin struck a match and lit an adjacent candle.

"Is this where you sleep?" I asked.

"This is where *ya* will sleep," he explained. "This will be suitable for ya, a girl."

Grin pulled a hidden blanket from the floorboards and tossed it my way.

"I'll be here early, and we'll go to newspaper row."

Grin made his way back to the hatch.

"Wait." I urged.

He stopped.

"There's so much I want to ask you."

"Plenty of time for that," he smiled.

Then, with a simple nod, he closed the hatch behind him and was gone.

I pulled the blanket over me and sat in the hushed attic of the church. It was small and cramped, but if I didn't think too hard, I wasn't scared. At least I was free of the asylum and free to imagine of a way to rescue Papa.

Chapter V

Vincent Boys

Morning came quickly. I was pleased that I awoke naturally and was ready to go when Grin tapped on the hatch. He had not changed a bit, and his clothes were still stained and dirty.

We didn't have to go very far. St. Paul's Chapel was situated right at Park Row, or Newspaper Row, where all major newspapers had their downtown offices. Even though the sun was barely up, there were hoards of newsboys gathered, ready for the day.

"There's lots of papes to sell, but I only sell the *Journal*. One of the yella kid papes," Grin explained.

"Yella kid? What are the yella kid papes?"

"Not yella, yell-*ow*." Grin let the "o" roll off his tongue in an effort to be proper in pronunciation.

"Oh, yell-*ow*." I enunciated.

"So ya know the best papes in New York, Joseph Pulitzer's the *World* and William Randolph Hearst's the *Journal?*"

I nodded in agreement, although I really had no clue.

"Well, these boys hate each other," Grin explained further. "So a couple years ago, Hearst stole away the popular cartoonist who drew *Hogan's Alley* to draw the yellow kid for his pape. Ya know about it, right?"

I shook my head.

"Ya don't know about the yellow kid? Shaved head, lots of mischief?"

I shook my head again.

Grin continued, "Ah, well, the comic was printed in color, and the kid was all dressed in yella. Well, Pulitzer kept printin' *Hogan's Alley* even after Hearst started printin' the same comic called *The Yellow Kid*, a sign of their rivalry with each other. So, 'yellow kid papers' was the name some guy gave the two papes,. I never thought the comic was any good, myself."

A bell tolled, and the gate to the paper's circulation office opened.

"I only have my nickel," I said to Grin as the line got closer and closer to the delivery window of the *New York Journal.*

"If we're partners, we'll both work to sell the papes, and you pay me back the cost of what ya sell."

I wanted to ask why Grin was helping me, but I was afraid I wouldn't get a truthful answer. At first thought, maybe he figured having a girl beside him would help him sell more papers, but Grin was too good of a newsie to need my help.

We approached the window of the counting room.

"Hundred papes." Grin smashed down sixty cents on the counter. The manager behind grunted and shoved the papers toward him.

"A hundred?" I asked as we walked away.

"That's just the morning pape," he explained.

It seemed like all boys knew Grin as they shouted "'Ello!" and "Mornin'!" when we walked past. But he kept to himself, just nodding to each one who greeted him.

"Do you prefer working alone?" I asked.

"Nah. Depends."

I tried not to appear eager as I followed behind him.

"You don't go to school?"

"School is here on the street. Why be locked up during the best time of the day?"

Grin walked quickly, moving up and across the street, passing the morning commuters with ease. He seemed like he had a plan, and I didn't question it.

"First thing you want to know about sellin', ya have to have a spot. Boys, and girls for that matter, are real territorial around here. Each gang has their spot. Most of the newsie girls are out by the bridge or up by the park."

"Are those good spots?"

"Some days. Morning is best at Wall Street, no two ways about it. Afternoon is best anywhere near the food. At night, it's the theaters. I keep moving, and since I have no one to depend on, no place to be, it's easy for me."

"You got me now."

He stopped. "Ya right, but you're like me. I see it in ya—you'll stand on your own soon."

As much as I wanted to take that as a compliment, there was a part of me that didn't want to leave Grin. I knew that if my poor attempts at selling the night before continued, maybe he wouldn't release me from training too quickly.

The businessmen of Wall Street emerged from the dawn like the mosquitoes in Chicago. They moved hurriedly, clouding the sidewalks as they rushed toward the white-columned buildings. Grin flew into action.

Unlike the smaller newsboys, Grin didn't shove the papers in the face of the men. He stood in one position, raised it high, and with confidence belted out the news of the day. His calm presence seemed to attract the men, who were turned off by the brash approach of the other newsboys. They swiftly bought the paper from Grin before continuing along their way.

As the chaos wore down, the other newsies started to take notice of me working with Grin.

"Who's the girl?" one sneered at Grin.

"Never ya mind." Grin shooed him off.

"She with you?"

"Yeah, what's it to ya?"

"I wouldn't be splittin' papes, especially now."

"What do ya mean?"

"The Long Island boys, didn't you hear?"

Grin shook his head.

"Strike fever, first Brooklyn Trolley strikers and now Long Island with newsboys."

"Strike?"

"Yes, um, I'm just tryin' to sell as many papes as I can today before it hits," the young boy said as he turned and ran off to a wealthy man stepping out of a carriage.

I looked at Grin. He was deep in thought.

"I've never seen you think so hard," I said lightly.

"We got to go."

"Where?"

"Vincent's," Grin said to himself.

I ran to catch up to Grin, who was already on the move. I remembered his mentioning the Vincent boys but had no idea what it meant. As we rounded Broadway onto Warren Street it became clear where we were headed: St. Vincent's Newsboy Home.

53 Warren Street was just two blocks from Newspaper Row. It looked like a religious boarding house, similar to the asylum. I was hesitant to approach.

"It'll be fine," Grin laughed. "We won't go inside."

Grin walked around back to the alley. Sure enough, there was a band of about ten boys, from ages ten and seventeen, gathered in secret. I wondered what it was about these particular boys that was enough to scare Rat off when Grin mentioned them.

The one leading the conversation had red hair and a black eye patch over his left eye.

"The Long Island boys had it right. The deliverymen was cheatin' 'em, givin' them a stack with a few papes less than their order. They had to soak 'em," said the boy with the eye patch.

A tall kid with a heavy brow and rather clean clothes leaned forward. "We don't need a strike. We all gotta eat. We all gotta pay board."

"But Abe, ever since de war, it's still six cents a ten. News ain't the same now, yet we are still payin' the same," said the boy sitting next to him, who looked older than most of the boys.

"I know what we pay, Jim," sneered Abe.

"It's Hearst and Pulitzer too. Both are stickin' to their price," added the smallest one of the group.

The leader took notice of Grin.

"Grin! Just in time."

"Kid." Grin spat in his hand, and the two shook. Kid's smile faded when he saw me.

"Why the dame?"

I didn't say anything.

"Why the strike?" Grin countered.

"Boot's takin' all his boys up to City Hall Park tomorra. Dave too. They'll make a decision there." Kid took a seat without recognizing my presence. I kept standing.

"We need to stand on our own no matter what," chimed in a stocky little boy with a very round face.

"We always do, Indian" Grin said.

A skinny boy chewing on a pretzel, lifted it in agreement,. "Cheers to that."

"It sounds like all gangs will be on their own, even if we do strike." Kid appeared to be the leader of the Vincent boys, and they hung on his every word.

"Will there be enough of us?" Grin challenged.

"There'll be a hundred boys at Park Row. That's enough to strike. I say we Vincents lead the cause, rally the others around us," another boy added.

"We ain't leadin' anythin' yet Fitz." Kid said, clearly annoyed by him. "But imagine Grin, if de Brooklyn boys are behind this, even Jersey."

"What about the cops?" Grin took the dice off the table between the boys and shook it in his hand.

"They're all tied up with the trolley strikers. They don't care 'bout us." The smallest boy interjected, now gnawing on half of the pretzel he seized from the tall skinny boy.

Grin nodded, taking this in.

"So, you with us?" Kid asked.

Grin rolled the dice: snake eyes.

"I'm with ya."

The boys turned and stared at me once more. Grin took note and spat again, shaking hands with Kid. "City Hall Park," Grin said.

As Grin and I walked off, I finally voiced my fear.

"Grin, I can't strike. I have to make money."

His face was serious.

"As much as I agree with ya, Elsie, I gotta do this. I want to help ya, but these boys know me. If I don't strike, I'm good as dead. But you're a girl. They won't soak ya."

"I can't sell without you."

"Imagine, though, if it works and we get the papes back to five cents a ten. That's about two dollars a month…" He seemed to lose his train of thought.

"Grin."

"I know, I'm sorry I got ya into this."

"I don't understand." I paused, still surprised with how quickly Grin agreed to the strike. "Who were those boys?"

"They're my brotherhood. Most know them around here as the Vincent Boys. The one with the eye patch is Kid Blink. Abe Newman, the one with the bushy eyebrows, he's actually got family on the East Side. He goes to school during the day, a smart kid. Next to him was Jim Gaiety, another sharp mutt. But he's all done with school, like me. Then there was the smallest one, Little Mikey, who never shuts up. He's a loyal kid, though. Ya could tell him anythin', and he'd take it to the grave. The annoying one next to Kid was Fitz. He's always got somethin' to say, even if he's got no idea what he's blabberin' about. Then there's Crazy Arborn. He was the lanky guy sittin' on the other side of Kid. He could be one of the best newsies if he wanted to be, but he sells pretzels. He just likes to hang with the Vincent Boys. Then there's the stocky round fella, Bob. We call him Indian."

"Why 'Indian'?"

"If ya heard how he sells his wares, ya wouldn't be askin'."

"And the other boys?"

"I hadn't seen them before." Grin stopped. "Hey, sorry I didn't introduce ya, but that's not how it works."

"How does it work?"

"Ya gotta prove yourself. But ya don't need to worry about that. Ya won't be strikin'. There're other papes you can sell without me."

Grin picked up the stack of papers on his shoulder. "Alright, I guess I got just one afternoon to show ya how to be a respectable newsie."

With Grin in the lead, we went on to sell papers, forgetting the impending strike.

Grin was right. Selling papers in the afternoon was better than any school lesson. The New York streets were alive with people more fascinating than any story in a school book.

Wandering through the shopping district with our papers, Grin was easily distracted by the shoestring peddlers and hand organists. Sometimes he would dance along to a hand organist, which brought on extra tips into the poor man's outstretched hat.

My favorite was the hokey-pokey carts, known for having the best ice cream.

"*O che poco!*" an Italian peddler shouted from his cart with a stripped awning. His phrase meant to explain "how little" the price of the ice cream was. Non-Italian customers thought "o che poco" sounded like "hokey pokey," and the name stuck.

Boys rushed to his cart with wide eyes. In a spirited manner, he scooped the ice cream and placed it on a clean white sheet of paper, handing it to a boy with a penny in return.

It wasn't just boys who flocked to his cart but neighboring peddlers who wanted relief from the hot summer air.

I licked my lips in envy as I watched them.

"I've never had some."

"Ya never had *gelato*!" Grin said in a boisterous fake accent.

Before I could say anything, Grin handed the man a penny and received his ice cream in return.

"For ya, my lady," he said, bowing and giving me the treat.

"Really? You can't afford…" Grin silenced me by shoving a wooden stick with a scoop of ice cream on the end into my mouth.

The flavors of gelato melted from a cool ice to a warm cream.

"Mmm…that's good!" I said.

"The many wonders of the street!" Grin sang.

We took off, laughing at the businessmen who tried to tap dance their way around the wound mechanical toys that rattled across the sidewalks. We sang along with the peddlers as they drew attention to their carts. We even tried to scare some of the Lord Fauntleroy boys in their spoiled rich outfits with tin snakes from the carts.

When we reached 23rd and 6th Avenue, Grin brought to my attention three young girls, around my age, with bright vibrant-colored hats, selling papers.

"Those are the Horn girls."

I immediately felt a twinge of jealously.

"They're good newsgirls. Everyone comes to see their hats. They have a lot of regulars."

"Do I need," I tried not to sound desperate, "a hat?"

He laughed. "No. Ya got very honest eyes. That should do."

The day continued with more rounds on the street. When Grin got his hundred papers for the evening edition, there were even more rumors about the City Hall Park meeting and strike. He casually ignored them.

At the theaters, he let me hawk some of the "papes." But as evening slowed down, we walked back downtown toward the church.

"We didn't sell our last twenty."

"That happens a lot these days, even with two newsies sellin'."

"Then what do you do?"

"Sometimes I head over to the meat yards. They'll buy the rest of the day-ol' papes for a few cents, to wrap the meat in."

"Oh."

"Ever since the war ended, most of the boys have been takin' a loss. We didn't spit about six cents a ten during the war, we were sellin' so good, but now it's hard. We expected the price of the pape to go back to five cents a ten like all the other papes and the way it was before the war. Now Pulitzer and Hearst are just being greedy, takin' the profit off our backs. That's why the boys want to strike."

"I understand. It's not fair."

Grin walked ahead.

"Is Vincent's where you sleep?" I finally asked when we closed in on the church.

"Sometimes."

"Do you have family?"

"Everybody's got somebody."

As we neared the church, it had an unusual glow from the inside. Grin turned to me and smiled. Whatever was inside cheered him up.

"Come on," he whispered.

We climbed into the attic, but what had been a quiet and dark church last night was now filled with a soft glow. From below came the most heavenly sound I had ever heard.

"What is it?" I asked in a low voice.

"The boys' choir."

The voices of the young boys blended into one another in perfect harmony, something I had never heard before.

Grin leaned back against the blanket, tucking his hands underneath his head and closing his eyes. I followed his lead. We sat in silence as the voices below carried through the thin floorboards, a private performance.

"They come here once a month."

"It's beautiful. I didn't know you like music," I teased.

He opened his eyes. "I like a lot of things. I think that's why the streets work so well for me. I see it all."

"You don't always want to be on the street, do you?"

"Did you know that the reverend who set up Vincent's also built a ranch out in Staten Island?"

"A ranch?"

"Yeah, and some of the boys, when they get old enough, can go out there, make a livin'."

Grin's eyes drifted off. "It's called Mount Loretto." He smiled. "It's a farm of about four hundred acres."

"Could you go now?"

"Soytenly, but I like it here on the streets for now. Farm life is just a thing to dream about."

The boys continued with a song in a language I couldn't understand, a secret, beautiful language.

"What do ya dream about?" he smiled back at me.

I was caught off guard. "Papa and me, getting him out."

Grin's face dropped. "I'm sorry…"

"No, it's alright. I know you didn't mean anything by it."

"Here I am carryin' on about things that don't matter. Look, I'll take you to the Tombs tomorra. But ya not gonnna go in, unless you wanna get carted back to that asylum."

I nodded. As the angelic voices below continued, I finally blurted, "Why are you helping me?"

His eyes drifted to the ceiling. The boys choir finished and the room fell silent.

"We're friends," he stated plainly.

In a swift movement, he was up and at the hatch.

"You don't need to tell me where you're going. I just want to know you'll be safe," I finally said.

"Ya never need to worry about me."

I wanted to insist, but I was too tired. Grin closed the hatch, and the attic was left in darkness.

All the heat and commotion of the day started to take its toll. I had never spent a whole day working in the sun, and I was exhausted. I wondered if I was even built for the streets like Grin was. But with the news of the strike, it was fair to think that tomorrow would be a different kind of day.

Chapter VI

The Tombs

"You're not coming," Grin insisted, eyes filled with anger at having to insist this for the fifth time.

"I just want to see what it is like," I pleaded. "And you can't stop me. I know where City Hall Park is."

Grin let out a groan and scratched his head under his cap, back and forth. "I'm not sure what these boys are up to. It could get rough."

"Then I'll leave."

The triangular plot of land known as City Hall Park was filled to the brim with newsboys. One in particular was standing like statue on the granite base of a pool that enclosed a two-tiered fountain.

As we approached, it became clear that he intended to stand like a statue, arms by his side and face turned up to the sky. Grin snickered.

"What?"

"Cohen is makin' himself look like Nathan Hale."

"Who?"

Grin pointed to a bronze statue at the other end of the park.

"He's a hero who died as a martyr durin' the revolutionary war. Cohen's far from any hero," Grin chuckled.

"Who is Cohen?"

"Morris Cohen, a guy with a big head. It's known that he always takes three hundred papes."

"Three hundred! And he sells them?" I was shocked.

"Well, he's not eatin' 'em. At least we don't think." Grin winked. I laughed.

As we blended with the crowd, an eleven-year-old boy by the name of Boots began his speech.

"It went dis way. We went to de bloke who sells de papers, and we tells him dat he got to be two fer a cent or nuthin'. He say, 'What are yer goin' do about it?' 'Strike,' sez I. The bloke sez, 'Go ahead and strike.' And here we is."

A boy by the name of Monix joined Boots' side to explain their argument. "The boys of Long Island City felt the *Journal* deliverymen was cheating them out of their money, giving them two papes short in their stack and things like that. So they gathered and tipped the wagons, running off with all the papes while others chased those deliverymen."

Newsboys cheered.

"But you see, it wasn't till after theys got in a bit of trouble that they realized who the real cheater was!" Monix shouted. "Hearst is stealin' pennies from our pockets while he lays his head on silk sheets."

"Pulitzer too!" shouted one of the voices from the crowd.

"Pulitzer too!" Cohen agreed. "I ain't no leader, but I do have a stake in this trade, and I say if I'm willing to lay down my three hundred papes a day till my brotherhood gets what they deserve, I say you alls do too!"

"See," Grin mocked, "a real martyr."

The boys cheered and raised their fists in the air. I admired their passion. I wondered if the streets made them this way or if they all were born with such spirit. I felt ashamed, as the boys fired on about their grievances, at how silent I was during the greatest injustices of my life. Maybe there was something I could have said to stop those cops from taking my pa.

Grin was tough to figure out. Here he insisted he had to go along with these boys, but he always made comments leading me to believe he wasn't one of them.

Grin's mystery was only enhanced by the fact that he didn't react like the other boys did to the numerous shouts of "five cents a ten" and "two fur a cent," even though I knew from my conversations with him that he felt the same way.

Kid Blink shot up beside Boots on the granite platform.

"What is the sense of this meetin'? Is it strike?"

"Strike!" echoed the boys.

"It's agreed. We strike, and we'll win before Dewey comes home!" shouted Kid.

The boys raised their hands in agreement. "Hooray for Dewey! Dewey our hero!"

"We all on strike!" Kid cheered. "Anyone sellin' de boycotted papes tomorra afternoon is a scab, and youse have every right to swipe their papes, tear 'em up, and throw 'em in the river."

A loud roar of cheers echoed from the park, and each passerby took note.

Kid went into action organizing the boys. "Jack, you and Boots take de demands to the papers, let 'em know what we strikin' for."

Jack nodded.

"Newsies, spread the good word to the Fifty-ninth Street boys, Harlem, Brooklyn, and Jersey!" shouted Kid.

It was entertaining to see how they worked. I figured most of them had probably learned the things to say and do from the Brooklyn Trolley workers, who had had their own fair share of strikes.

"Who's Dewey?" I asked Grin when he returned with strike circulars, written declarations that the newsboys were on strike, willing to sell any "pape" that wasn't the *Journal* or *World*.

"Don't know Dewey? Ya got a lot to learn!" shouted Grin in amazement. "First, we need to get you outta here."

In an instant, the Vincent boys emerged and Kid took Grin by the neck.

"We gonna be organizin' and formin' an executive strike committee," Kid said.

"I gotta do somethin' first, then I'll be there." Grin slipped out of Kid's grasp.

The boys eyeballed me. It was clear that they were not used to Grin turning them down, even for a minute.

"We'll meet you over at the spot," Kid finally said, and the boys hurried off with the crowd.

"What do you have to do?"

"I promised I'd show ya the Tombs," he said, leading me away from the mass of newsies.

"Dewey?" I reminded him.

Grin scoffed, "Admiral Dewey of the Navy! Single-handedly won the war. He's our hero, goin' to be comin' home to a hero's welcome by the end of the summer."

"So that's what Kid means by winning before Dewey comes home?"

"Well," Kid smiled, scrunching up his face, "Kid kind of says it for everythin'. But in this case, it fits," he laughed.

As we walked out of the park, I took notice of the bronze sculpture of Nathan Hale. Written underneath was an inscription: "I regret I have but one life to lose for my country." It was a beautiful statue, and I was sure that without the newsboys and their strike, I would have never have noticed it was ever there.

"Come on." Grin shoved me forward, desperately trying to dodge the swarming newsies.

At every chance he got, Grin belted news of the strike and handed out his flyers. Some people were even kind enough to hand us change in support of our cause. By the time we reached the Tombs, we had earned fifteen cents. It was a good profit for half a day's work.

My elation at our quick profit was deflated at the sight of our destination. The Tombs was everything Grin hinted it was, a fortress. Its design, people said, looked Egyptian, so they named it "the Tombs." Rumor had it that the jail was built on a filled-in pond and had eventually sunk a few feet into the ground—another reason for the nickname. Grin added that it was full of corrupt cops and a place you never wanted to find yourself in.

"Now, I know a guy in there. That's how I was able to learn about your pa. They do allow visitors, but I'm afraid, that if we walk in and say who ya are, they'll be on ya quick. This is the first place that Asylum would come lookin' for ya."

"What do we need to do?" I asked.

"Least now ya know where he is." Grin pointed to a courthouse next door. "He'll be tried there in those courts. I figure I can go in and find out when that will be."

"I wish I could see him…"

"Oh, spit…" Grin mumbled under his breath as he backed away from me.

I turned and saw the purpose of his recoil. The Vincent Boys were crossing Leonard Street, heading our way. Their arms crossed, they looked like they had a score to settle. Grin stood between the boys and me.

"We got a problem, Grin?"

"Nah."

"What's goin' on?"

Grin grit his teeth, then buckled. "Her pa's inside the Tombs."

"Ghad awful place," spat Fitz. "My uncle was there two years until they let him out. He said it was hell."

I swallowed hard.

"That was a few years ago. It's only five years old now. How bad can it smell?" asked Little Mikey.

"She yer friend then?" Kid interrupted, staring at Grin.

"Yeah," Grin answered back, unfolding his arms.

It was hard for me to hide my smile at his declaration.

Kid stepped up to me and looked me over. Grin kept close by. Then to my surprise, Kid spat on his hand and stuck it out to me. "Then youse got de brotherhood," he said.

It looked like Grin wanted to step in and say something, but he held himself back. Without a second thought, I spat in my hand and shook the tall boy's outstretched symbol of acceptance.

"We won't treat youse like a girl."

"I don't want you to," I spat back.

The boys laughed. "Alright then, let's get youse inside," Kid said.

"What?"

"No," Grin objected. "They'll be lookin' for her."

"That don't matter," Kid huffed.

"You can get me inside?" I said eagerly to Kid as Grin stepped between us.

"It's too dangerous."

"She's part of de brotherhood, so eithers youse get her in or I will."

Grin looked at me, and I pleaded. "Please?"

"Fine," Grin relented.

The boys concocted that they would make a distraction, but in order for it to work, I would have to look like a boy.

"Fitz, youse give her your cap and trousers," Kid ordered.

"What!" Fitz shot back.

"She can sneak in better lookin' like a boy, and youse looks like a good fit."

"What's am I suppose to wear, the dress?" The boys doubled over in laughter.

Kid took hold of Fitz and whipped off his cap, tossing it to me. Fitz uttered a few colorful remarks and then slipped off his trousers, standing on the corner in his dingy white undergarments.

Fitz's clothes were surprisingly a good fit. I tucked my dress into the trousers and my hair underneath the cap.

Grin laughed, "The look does suit ya."

Two guards held watch outside of the pillared entrance to the Tombs. My heart pounded as we approached. Their faces matched the stone of the building, and I thought at any moment they would break. Slowly one of the guards' chins began to turn my way, and I held my breath.

Bang!

Behind us, Kid collided with Abe in a fistfight full of swearing and accusations. The stone-faced guards quickly moved to break them up.

"Are they okay?" I questioned.

"Shh!" Grin hushed. "It's our distraction."

I felt foolish as we hurried quickly up the steps of the jailhouse. Inside, the shadowed darkness of the building engulfed us. Grin took my hand and hurried me along the wall down a hallway. I figured we were making a run for the jail cells, although I had no idea in this maze where we were.

All of sudden, he made a sharp detour into what looked like an office. A constable with a large barrel chest and a square jaw immediately stood when we entered.

"What in God's—!"

"It's me!" Grin tipped up his hat, revealing his face.

The round man roared with laughter. "You gave me a fright, little Grinnan."

I smiled. Grin's real name had finally been revealed.

"Whose ya friend?"

"Nickel," Grin spat out without a beat. I prayed silently that I passed as a boy.

The man seemed less concerned with me as he walked over to Grin.

"What can I do fer ya?"

"The man I saw before—I need to see him again."

"Does this man owe ya money? If so, I can swear he has none on 'im."

"Nah, information."

"I'll get it outta him," he said sinisterly, pounding his fist into his hand.

"No!" I blurted out. I corrected myself and dropped my voice to sound like a boy. "No. We need to hear it ourselves."

The plump cop considered for a moment. "Alright."

The cop went to his desk and grabbed two pieces of paper and handed them over to us.

"Don't lose these," he insisted.

I examined the piece of paper. It was a visitor pass, the name field blank. I preferred it that way.

In the next instant, we were in the most hideous place, deep in the bowels of the Tombs, filled with mold, damp and dreary. We descended into the men's jail, a narrow room with a high ceiling and a series of four floors of wrought iron cells. I dared not touch anything as we moved up a set of stairs to the second floor.

"Second floor is for murders." The cop explained. "Here we are."

The three of us stopped in front of a small cell. I looked in but could not recognize my Papa.

"Lutz!" Grin shouted.

Suddenly, a figure arose from the darkness. He was frail and dirty. His eyes were sunken in, and he walked toward the bars like he was dragging a ton of steel behind him. My heart broke. It took every inch of me not to cry and break the deception of my disguise.

"Alright, there's our man." The plump cop made his way back down the stairs. "Don't stay too long, I don't want to be responsible for ya catching fever."

"Thank you, Noches!" Grin shouted back.

When our escort was out of earshot, Grin continued, "Dietrich Lutz?"

"*Was* do you want, boy?" My father's voice was harsh and cold.

I edged closer and removed my cap, letting my hair fall down around my shoulders. Papa was confused but edged closer. His eyes widened. "Elsie?"

"Papa."

"Elsie, *was*…what…"

"I'm gonna save you."

"How?" He coughed. "I sick. Very sick."

"When is your trial?"

Papa shook his head. "In a few days?"

"What can I do?"

Papa was silent; then he shook his head again. "*Nichts.*"

He coughed again. Grin took my arm.

"What's wrong with him?" I asked Grin in a low voice.

"Many die in here from typhoid fever, a third reason for the nickname Tombs."

"No," I stated flatly. I wasn't going to believe it. "There has to be something I can do."

"What is your name?" Papa turned and asked Grin.

Grin removed his cap and stood up straight. "Henry Grinnan, sir."

"Take care of her," Papa spoke. Then he turned to me. "Be good, a good girl."

"No, I don't want to say goodbye."

"Oh, Elsie." Papa reached out and touched the tears streaming down my face. "*Ich bin* happy you are alright."

"I can't live without you, Papa."

"You boys there!" shouted a voice from down the hallway.

Grin turned to me. "Hurry! Put your cap on."

Quickly, I stuffed my hair under my cap.

"Here, take this. Buy some food." Grin hurried, taking two dollars out of his pocket and handing it to my pa. "We gotta run."

"But…"

"Come on."

The lone voice from the end of the hallway emerged with a flood of footsteps. We had to hurry. I took one last look at my father. He tried to smile, but it wasn't convincing. "*Ich liebe dich.*"

"I love you too." The words flew out of my mouth as Grin dragged me by the arm back through the maze and away from the descending horde of cops.

The voices and shouting got closer with every turn through the cells, but we were smaller and moved faster through the aisles than the men did. Within a few seconds, Grin and I were back at Noches's office and, with a few more steps, out the door.

Grin and I ran so fast to the other side of the street that the afternoon traffic acted as a curtain closing behind us. The midday rush of commuters shielded us from the dazed pair of cops, who scanned the crowd from the tops of the steps of the Tombs.

Grin stopped to catch his breath. I felt I had left mine inside.

"Are ya okay?" he panted.

I nodded, tucking my hands into the pants of my borrowed trousers so Grin couldn't see that they were shaking.

"I knew it wouldn't help…" Grin sighed.

"No, it's not that. I just don't want to talk about it right now."

Many emotions were swirling inside me, but the most prominent one was fear. I didn't know what I would do now. Every time I even thought about my options, my mind drifted back to the asylum, and I refused to make that my only choice.

I looked at Grin. His eyes were focused on the ground.

"Who was that cop?"

Grin looked up at me.

"Eddie Noches. He worked with my pa."

"Your father was a cop?"

"*Is* a cop. Uptown."

The Vincent boys, busy handing out flyers on the corner of Centre Street, cheered when they saw us.

"Did you make it?" Mikey asked, running over.

I nodded.

They could tell by the expression on Grin's and my faces it wasn't good news, and Kid changed the subject, taking me by the shoulder. "So, looks like we gotta new boy. We should initiate."

The boys cheered. I looked to Grin, who shook his head.

"She's not part of us."

For the first time, I felt anger toward Grin. "You can't tell me what I can do."

"Elsie," Grin whispered, pulling me aside, "I'm just tryin' to explain to them that ya can't strike."

I looked deep into Grin's eyes. He was trying his best to help me, but after the asylum and the way Pa looked at me in the Tombs, I was certain that the kind of help Grin was suggesting was not the help I needed. I didn't want to be afraid anymore, and these boys were the most confident people I had ever known.

"I want to be part of the brotherhood," I stated.

Grin looked at me with stern eyes. "Ya don't know what you're sayin'."

I pushed Grin aside.

"I'm part of your brotherhood," I said. "I'm fit as any of you, and I'm ready to strike."

Kid smiled at Grin. "Looks like youse found yourself some trouble."

Grin, fuming with anger, didn't say anything.

"Only fittin', we all about trouble here." Kid smiled. "De rest of the boys are gonna be talkin' about de strike and makin' plans. So should we."

They all agreed.

"Let's go to Mitchell's. We'll plays craps for who pays."

The boys cheered.

Grin took me by the wrist. "Let's just go."

"Why?"

"Look, ya not one of them."

"You mean I'm not with you. You're with them."

"'Cause I gotta be."

"If I don't, you don't."

Grin gritted his teeth. Something about this he didn't like. "Ya a girl. God made you that way."

"If boys' clothes are good enough to get me past the Tombs guards, they'll do for all the rest. Besides, I have nowhere else to go."

Grin thought for a moment. "I show ya a good place, for a girl. I'd show ya now if ya want."

I could tell he was trying to think of every way to convince me not to strike with the Vincents.

"Grin, after seeing my father like that...I got nothing. If they want to be my family now, I want to be theirs."

"They ain't your family, Elsie. These boys can be...they're not good."

"Let me decide that."

I wrenched my hand out of his grip and walked in my britches and cap to join the brotherhood.

Chapter VII

Brotherhood

"Craps. Game of dice, game of luck," Fitz explained, now dressed in a fine replacement of clothes, a stolen messenger boy's jacket and a potato-sack skirt.

I'm sure he expected to receive his clothes after we'd gotten through the Tombs, but Kid insisted I keep them and christened them my new clothes while adopting Grin's nickname for me, Nickel—the exact amount of money I earned on my first night hawking "papes" with him on the White Way.

Fitz shook the dice in his hand and rolled them on our table at Mitchell's Diner.

The next to explain the rules was Abe. "Seven or eleven, that's good. You want that."

Grin rolled his eyes as he sat on the edge of the booth. "Don't play any games of chance with these thieves."

"That's only 'cause you got no luck, Grin," Fitz laughed.

"And ya got no money. I say we're even."

Fitz snarled.

"Look, boys," Kid started in, "tomorra we gonna set out our demands, fifty cents a hundred like it was before the war."

"I don't understand. Why did they raise it to sixty cents?" I asked.

"'Cause they could," sniffed Grin. "You see, during the war, everyone was buyin' papes to find out what was happenin' every hour. Hearst and Pulitzer were lickin' it up like dogs, puttin' out extra editions an' everythin'. Some say they must have started the war themselves, just so they could make a profit. Since they were competin' with themselves, neither of them was willin' to raise the price of the pape on the customer—"

"So they raised it on the newsie," Kid cut Grin off, fuming with anger.

"Why didn't anyone say anything then?"

The boys grumbled.

"We were makin' the money then, sellin' all the papes, rarely had a hitch. I think we all expected it to go back down to two for a cent," explained Jim Gaiety, the oldest newsie of the bunch at seventeen. "Now we never know how many papes we gonna sell, and if we buy too many—well, that's just our fault."

The waitress slammed down fresh, steaming red hots on our table. It was a mouth-watering sight to see those delicious sausages tucked in bread rolls. The boys reached out for them in haste.

"Just 'cause we're striking doesn't mean we should be starvin'," Mikey said as he stuffed the meat and bun into his mouth.

I paused. I didn't want to take the red hot if I couldn't pay. But as I considered and battled with my growling stomach, Grin shoved it my way.

"Eat," he demanded.

"I can't—"

He cut me off. "Eat. I am lucky, no matter what they say."

Sure enough, Grin was lucky. He threw two sevens in a row and saved us from paying for our meal.

As we walked back to the church, Grin was silent.

"I wish you'd tell me what's wrong with you."

He merely shrugged. I was still pursuing him when a couple passed and the woman threw a harsh glance my way. I instinctively wiped my face, thinking that was the culprit. Grin nudged my shoulder.

"It's your clothes."

I had completely forgotten that I was still wearing Fitz's hand-me-downs and was perfectly content to never take them off. They were more comfortable and easy to get around in.

"You don't like me tagging along with the Vincents."

"No," he said flatly.

"Why?"

"*I* don't like taggin' along with the Vincents," he said, feeling that was a good enough explanation.

"But they were the first guys you ran to when you heard about the strike, and you said yourself, you're one of them."

"'Cause I gotta be."

"Why?"

"I owe them. Look," he turned to me and tipped his cap up so I could see in his eyes that he was serious, "the Reformers are right when they say the streets are no place for a girl. They're rough out here, so ya have to have a gang. I'm pretty tough, but even I'm not stupid enough to roll around without protection."

"But it's not just that. You said you owe them."

"I did."

"And you're not going to tell me why?"

"Nope."

"So I suppose you're not going to tell me about that book in the back of your trousers, either?"

"Ya never asked about that." His eyebrows lifted.

"Wait, so you gonna tell me?"

He paused, then smiled. "No."

"Argh!" I let out a huff.

He laughed and then stopped abruptly, his eyes were fixed straight ahead.

"What?" I turned in the direction of his gaze only to see five newsboys approaching. As they got closer, I could see the towering leader and his dripping greasy hair. It was Rat.

"Wells, wells, wells, what have we here?" he said, his lips flapping over his gums like an old dog.

"A boy and a half," said one of his henchmen, signaling that I was the "half."

"I thought you took up with no one, Grin?"

"I remember I said I didn't take up with vermin—that'd be ya of course."

Rat flung his body forward, a threat. Grin didn't budge.

"So I hears they whisperin' strike? What says you?"

One of the henchmen eyed me as the conversation between Rat and Grin escalated. At that moment I remembered I wanted Grin to teach me how to fight.

"If they strike, I strike."

"Pity," Rat mumbled.

"Better not let them here ya say that."

"Why? We ain't scared. I'm sure we gonna have some muscle on our side. I think it'd be a good fight."

"Not an even one!" A voice came from behind us.

Kid and the Vincent boys moved up to stand with Grin and me. Rat slowly backed away. I didn't know whether it was from fear or just to be closer to his own boys.

"Ah, Kid, the one-eyed mutt. Long time."

"Ain't it great that it wasn't long enough." Kid cracked his knuckles.

"I lookin' forward to tomorra, Kid, when me and my boys get the pickin' from the beautiful New York streets." Rat stretched out his hands like he was embracing the immense city.

"Youse gonna have a thousand fists starin' right back at cha," Kid interjected.

Rat laughed, "Everyone's out for themselves. It's how it's always been. Even Grin knows that."

I didn't like Rat singling out Grin. It made me aware that they all knew way more about him than I did.

"This time it's different," Grin began. "We are all gonna have a union."

"Who youse foolin'?" Rat spat back. "The money youse lose will be more than a penny a ten. And the money I make, I'll be dinin' with Will and Joe."

"Hard to sell shredded papes, Rat," said Kid. "And we got Dave on our side. Prizefighter of the Union."

"I ain't afraid of Simmons." Rat spat on the ground. "I'm markin' ya, Grin. Fair fight tomorra. Youse better not have ya girl too close. She gonna get hurt too." Rat pointed his finger at me. It wobbled in the air. In an instant, I hacked up some mucus in the back of my throat and spat at Rat. It landed below his eye on his upper cheek.

The Vincent boys roared with laughter and jeers. Rat wiped the spit off with a sleeve that hung long past his hand and edged close to me. Grin put out his arm.

"I ain't a nice boy, miss. I'd soak a lady."

Grin shoved Rat back away from me. "I'd like to see you try."

The two stood in tense silence.

"Tomorra, Rat," Kid echoed casually, a wooden toothpick from Mitchell's hanging out of his mouth, "if you stills thinkin' of being a scab."

Rat snorted and turned on his heels. His boys followed him off down the street. Fitz patted my shoulder. "Good work, Nickel."

"It looks like we gotta have a strategy now," Kid said, all business, "if newsies are already thinkin' of being scabs."

"Rat ain't hard to take care of. Or his crew," Mikey said.

Grin shook his head. "They're right, though. The papes will hire muscle. Gutter monkeys like Rat will try to hide behind 'em."

"Well, we'll use our brains. I know Dave and Morris, and they are makin' plans. If we can get Brooklyn, it'll be a walk."

All the newsboys agreed.

"Wait," I said as the boys started to head off.

They turned, eager for what I had to say.

"I'm part of you, right?"

They nodded.

"Well..." I stressed, "I got to know how to fight."

The boys rolled with laughter, getting a real kick out of this. For the next few blocks, Crazy A and Abe each took pretend swings and jabs as Mikey demonstrated his defense routine. Grin wasn't pleased and didn't bother participating, folding his arms into his chest.

"All in all, kick between the legs," Mikey suggested as we arrived the well-lit building of the Newsboy Home on Canal Street. "Just kick between the legs."

"You're not gonna be fightin'," Grin whispered in my ear as the boys filed into the house.

"I might not have a choice."

"Not if I'm around."

Grin walked ahead, escorting me back to my church.

"You'll get caught," he explained reasonably. "It won't be hard for them to spot a girl. You're the first one the cops will take."

"Not if I am dressed in my trousers and cap," I reasoned.

"I'm not one to tell you no; I'm not your pa."

"No, you're not," I said somberly.

"I'm sorry, I didn't mean to mention—"

"It's okay. I know."

I climbed up into the attic. Grin paused at the hatch. I thought for a moment he would explain everything. But he didn't.

"I won't fight," I said. "I mean, I won't know how."

Grin simply nodded and descended down the hatch.

That night, I couldn't sleep at all. The minute I closed my eyes, a terrible nightmare played out before me.

I was lost in sea of striking newsboys, all running and trampling forward as I fought against the tide, screaming for Papa.

As I rounded the corners of the crowded streets, the dense population of boys grew scarce, and a lone man was sitting on an empty barrel. It was Papa. As I approached, his head was in his hands, and he began to mumble softly in German.

In an instant, his eyes flew open. His shirt was open on his chest, the hideous red circles of typhoid fever clustered on his skin. His sunken eyes looked right past me.

"Papa," I cried, but he didn't respond.

As I edged closer, his mumbling became clearer. But it wasn't his voice; it was my mother's: "Be strong. Speak up." Her voice, through my father's lips, repeated again and again, "You have a loud voice...loud. Be strong and speak up...loud. Elsie, Elsie, Elsie."

I gasped for air as I awoke in the stillness of the attic with sweat beading on my forehead.

My heart pounded. I tried desperately to slow my breathing, to calm myself, but the emptiness of the room only heightened my fear. The only reassuring comfort was the fact that Papa was still alive. There had to be some hope in that. "Calm, Elsie," I said to myself. "Don't cry. Don't cry," I repeated. "He's still alive. Papa is still alive."

Chapter VIII

Strike

I didn't mention my dream to Grin, but it lingered like a storm cloud above my head and weighed me down.

"Are ya alright?" he asked, figuring my sour look was my fear of what was to come with the strike. And although that wasn't the sole reason, it was enough of a partial truth.

"Yes, I'm fine."

As we approached Newspaper Row, I secured my hair under my cap. The sight before me, however, nearly stopped me dead in my tracks. Grin, too, faltered.

A hundred newsboys with banners, placards on their hats, and badges on their shirts had gathered outside of the gates, but not with intent to buy the papers. They were intent on stopping them. Almost every boy had a badge that read, "I ain't a scab." In the hands of a few were thick red clubs like the spokes of a wagon wheel. The fact that the boys felt they needed clubs put a pit in my stomach.

The Vincent boys saw us approach and held out our two badges. I earnestly took mine and pinned it on.

"We'll move toward de middle," Kid exclaimed. "They are gonna release de delivery wagons, but we can't do much until they arrive at de points."

"But we already got 'em scared," Fitz said with a smirk, "The windowman is pacin', shiverin' in his boots. They ain't even opened the gates yet. They scared."

"We gonna follow de wagon up to Fifty-ninth, stop the delivery," Kid continued, annoyed that he was rudely interrupted. "Jack is going to take his boys downtown."

"I'm not goin' uptown." Grin stated flatly.

"I'll be alright," I interjected, but it seemed it had nothing to do with me.

Kid was about to speak but then stopped. The two shared eye contact, an understanding between them.

"We'll rethink then," Kid finally said. "Dave!"

Up walked the famous Dave that Kid kept talking about. Grin shook his hand in a familiar way.

"Heard you won the fight last night," Grin congratulated.

Dave nodded with pride. He clearly thought highly of himself. To me, however, the boy looked far from a "prizefighter." He just looked like a regular old newsie.

The circulation bell sounded, and the roar of the thousand boys who hollered at its toll sent chills up my spin.

A handful of boys began to file through the opening gate in a hurry, anxious to get away from the mob and take possession of their papers.

Shouts of "Scab!" echoed through the open street. To my surprise, a small group of women followed the boys.

"Oh, I see, mongrel! Having the ladies do your dirty work!"

I turned to Grin. "Are they going to hurt those women?"

Grin shook his head, "I don't think so."

"Five cents a ten!" some boy shouted from the crowd. His roar spread, and the phrase grew into a chant. "Five cents a ten! Five cents a ten! Five cents a ten!"

The scabs returned to the edge of the gate. They didn't look like hired muscle but regular newsboys. I figured they were newsies, just like me, who couldn't afford to miss one day of work. I turned to Grin. "Maybe they don't know that if we all stick together for even a day, it won't last long."

"They know," Grin said as the scabs proceeded past the open gate and onto the streets. The boys were immediately pounced upon. The flood of striking newsies descended on the scabs, ripping their papers to shreds.

Grin held me toward the back of the crowd as Kid and the boys entered the fight. A few more delivery wagons exited the gate, and the strikers split up to follow.

Grin was right. This was not a scene I was comfortable in. The strikers flew like wild demons after the delivery trucks, howling at the tops of their lungs. They lunged at the carts but only succeeded in stopping one when the shaken driver abandoned his seat and ran back into the distribution center. Boys with clubs repeatedly knocked the gates, causing the few scabs who had yet to advance past them to shred up their own papers, which ignited cheers from the strikers.

Suddenly, a whistle hailed from behind the crowd, and cops flooded the scene. Grin grabbed my hand and pulled me behind the side of the building.

"I thought they'd be with the trolley strikers?" I asked, confused.

Just then the Vincent boys flew around the corner.

"Come on!" Kid yelled as we fled with them. A delivery wagon passed us unharmed.

Once we were safely around the corner, Kid took Grin aside. "If we gonna stop the papes, we got to go to the distribution points."

A man in a top hat passed us on his way to work. "Keep up the good work, boys!"

The boys shouted and cheered, throwing their fists in the air.

The man responded by tossing a quarter high, and the boys fought over it like a gold nugget.

"Kill the scab!" rang out from the boys, and a kid with papers tucked under his arm ran for his life. Kid and Grin did not take notice, as they were in deep conversation.

Boots approached and took Kid by the shoulder, breaking up his and Grin's discussion. "They gots five hundred boys up at Fifty-ninth. That's where the action is. You comin?"

Kid turned and looked at Grin, whose arms were folded across his chest. He looked at me. Finally, Grin gave in and nodded.

"Yeah," Kid nodded.

I could tell this was not Grin's decision.

"Come on then!" Boots shouted as he led a crowd up the street.

Mikey must have noticed my confused look as we wandered up Broadway toward the distribution point at 59th and Columbus Circle.

"Grin doesn't go pas' Fiftieth," he said casually.

"Why?" I shot back inquisitively.

Mikey shrugged his shoulders.

"So why does Kid care? He can go without him."

Mikey shook his head and smiled. "Kid needs Grin."

"I don't understand."

"Grin knows everyone!" Mikey said, surprised I didn't know.

I didn't know what Mikey meant; I had never seen anyone on the streets call out Grin by name but newsies.

"He got you into Tombs, didn't he?" he smirked.

"Yeah but...?"

"He knows as many people as the mayor, but he likes pretendin' he don't."

"Why, why..." Words were stumbling as I tried to understand. "Grin keeps to himself. I never see him talking to anyone."

"He doesn't have to. The people he knows are the important ones. At least it seems. They don't want to be seen talkin' with a newsie."

"Oh. Then why does Grin need Kid?"

"I ain't figured that one out yet," Mikey responded tapping his head to suggest he would put his brain to it.

I watched Grin as he headed with his badge and banner, shouting with the other boys as they marched up the avenue. "Don't buy the *Journal* and *World*! Newsboys on strike!"

Now with this latest revelation about Grin, he was even more of a mystery, which frustrated me.

The numbers of the streets continued to climb: 31st, 39th, until 48th.

"Scab!" shouted Kid, pointing to a boy selling papers on the corner of 48th and Broadway.

"Wait, wait, wait!" Abe shouted as he held back furious newsies with one hand. "We don't know he's sellin' the yellow kid papes."

"Look at him!"

The boy was built like a horse. In fact, he didn't look like a boy at all. His body was like a coal digger, with broad shoulders and thick, monstrous legs. Even if this boy was a scab, he was not to be messed with.

"Who is he?" the boys asked each other, but no one knew him.

"You all check it out. We'll keep goin' uptown," Dave said to Kid.

Kid cracked his knuckles, and Fitz handed him a club. The boys continued up the street. I looked to Grin, expecting relief at not crossing his imaginary boundary, but he was just intent on the situation, giving me no signs that would further decode his mystery.

"I don't like this," Grin said, speaking up. "He can't be alone."

"Let's find out," Kid said, ignoring him and moving on toward the mule. "Hey, youse there!" Kid yelled.

The boy didn't turn. His ears seemed as dense as his muscle.

"Whatcha sellin'?" Fitz called, eager for a fight.

The boy finally turned and set his eyes on the six of us. He merely squinted and then said, "What do you care?"

"If ya sellin' boycotted papes, we got a problem with it."

"The *World* and *Journal*?" the boy looked around in a gloating manner. "They on strike, ain't they?"

"Then let me see." Kid eased in, close enough to smell the boy's festering sweat. "I'm lookin' to buy me a yella kid pape."

"Then it's ya lucky day."

Without a single word more, Kid and Fitz lunged at the boy while Mikey swiped his papers and ripped them to shreds. I pulled my cap lower over my eyes as I watched the boy suspiciously refuse to fight back.

Suddenly, a whistle blew and a sea of constables emerged and encircled us. The thick mule of a boy smirked in pleasure as he finally flung the three boys off of him.

"It's a trap!" Grin shouted, grabbing my arm. We tried to get away, but the cops surrounded us.

I tried to keep my head down so they wouldn't recognize me as a girl, but it was hard to see where everyone was going. The boys scattered every which way. Grin and I broke out and started running down the alley, a cop hot on our tail.

We ducked around back to a fire escape. Grin hopped up and then held out his hand for me. I struggled with the rungs of the ladder, my boots barely hanging on, when he finally pulled me up with all his might.

We tucked ourselves around the stairs of the second flight and watched as the cop looked up and down the alley. In an instant he was back out on the street.

"Follow me," Grin said, signaling to climb higher.

At the top of the building, we had a clear view of the city baking in the summer heat.

I peered over the side of the building, down toward the street below. Grin joined my side. Despite our position, we could the officers arrest Fitz, no other boys in sight.

"We're arresting you for disturbing the peace." The policeman spoke in an official manner.

"Like I could ever lick that mule!" Fitz shot back.

The mighty boy shrugged his massive shoulders and chuckled a deep throaty laugh.

Grin shook his head. "Poor Fitz."

"The cops set a trap!" I was shocked.

Grin shook his head. "Nah, it was Hearst, or one of his men. They wanted to catch a newsie in action. Take 'em in, book 'em…ya know, make an example. They're just tryin' to scare us."

"But there's so many newsies."

"Yeah, it won't work. Not many cops out today anyway. The newsies were smart to start now."

"You mean 'we.'"

Grin turned to me and looked for a second, then smiled. "Yeah, sure. 'We.'"

Chapter IX

William Randolph Hearst

That night, the newsboy leaders formed an executive
strike committee, set up to organize and negotiate the
terms of the strike. Kid Blink was the chief organizer,
Dave Simmons became the president for his notoriety,
and Mikey was commissioned the orator. Abe and Jim
were summoned to serve as the brains of the operation,
and Monix was tapped for his passion, joined by a few
other boys from different districts: Crutchy, Scabooch,
and Barney Peanuts.

Grin didn't nominate himself but stayed quiet
through the whole ordeal. Kid and Dave were the real
stars of the evening and quietly became the clear leaders,
much to the dislike of Jack Sullivan and Boots, both of
whom helped organize the rally the day before.

The real seal of the union's legitimacy came when
Brooklyn newies arrived at the meeting under the
leadership of Spot Conlon and Racetrack Higgins. Spot,
the "Grand Master Workboy of Brooklyn," as he was

called, singled out Kid as the "Grand Master Workboy of Manhattan" and pledged their support. Racetrack vowed they would be there in the morning to soak scabs and would strike until "two fer a cent."

One of the more colorful newies I met that night was Young Myers, or Mush, as they called him, for the way he flirted with the ladies. Needless to say, he quickly sought me out of the bunch for lively conversation.

"Okay, Mush, Elsie and I have to go." Grin edged in between us.

"Tomorra you shouldn't be fightin' with those tender hands." Mush smiled, edging closer to me. "You should be treated to a nice dinner at the Broadway Central Hotel."

"Okay, Mush!" Grin shouted so loud in my ear that it vibrated with a ringing sound.

Mush lifted up his hands in surrender and backed down. I looked at Grin, amused. "Don't think it's anything special. He flirts with all girls like that."

"I didn't say anything," I smirked.

In the morning, Grin revealed that he had strike committee business for us that morning and we shouldn't join the other boys on Park Row.

"Where are we going?"

Grin was silent as he jogged through the streets. My shoes, never faithful to my feet, slipped and slid, but Grin never ran ahead. He always kept an eye out as I stopped to bend over and tie the laces tighter around my soles.

"Are we going to the distribution point?"

Again, Grin ignored me and kept walking.

"I'd wish you just teach me how to swing. I'd catch on quick and then you wouldn't worry."

"It's not ya I worry about. It's boys like Rat who truly would soak a girl."

Grin made his way to 6th Avenue then descended down 23rd Street.

"Aren't you going to tell me where we're going?"

Grin pointed ahead of him to a large building with at least twenty stories.

"What's in there?"

"A lawyer."

"We need a lawyer for the strike?"

"No, we need a lawyer for your pa."

I stopped, "What?"

"Ya may have given up, but I haven't. There's always a way," Grin insisted, continuing ahead. "Ya comin'?" He waved, seeing I had not budged an inch.

The strike had let me forget my dream from the previous night, but now I wasn't sure that was a good thing.

"Trust me," Grin insisted again, holding out his hand.

I placed my small hand in his outstretched rough and calloused palm. "I trust you."

Grin proceeded to the elevator of the pristine building. I paused to marvel. I had never been in an elevator before and was stuck admiring the curious closet-like contraption's metal panels, elaborately worked with swirling designs.

"Ya scared?" Grin asked, confusing my awe for anxiety.

"Nah...No," I stumbled out, stepping into the elevator.

Grin laughed and slid a metal gate across us, latching it closed.

"So Mikey was right," I said low under my breath.

"Why, what did Mikey say?"

"That you know everyone, everyone important."

"Nah, I don't"

Grin pulled out the book in his back trousers, opened it slightly, and a card fell out. It read *Walter Trough, attorney at law, 10ᵗʰ floor, 601 W. 23ʳᵈ Street.* "I found it in a gutter," Grin chuckled, grabbing a lever attached to a round metal box and pulling it back. The elevator rumbled and then ascended with a slow clicking. I braced myself against the corner. Grin smiled, his hand securing the lever, perfectly content in control of the moving box.

"How do you know how to do that?" I asked.

"Saw a guy once."

The elevator's front bars allowed us to see numbers on the wall marking the floors as we ascended. As soon as we rolled passed the ninth floor, Grin slowly pushed the lever back to the center and we stopped. Proud of his operation of the elevator, he smirked as he slid open the gate and stepped out onto the tenth floor.

It wasn't hard to find the office: "Walter Trough, Attorney at Law" was clearly written on the door in bold black letters.

Without hesitating, Grin walked right in. A secretary looked up from a typewriter.

"May I help you?" she sneered.

"We're here to see a lawyer."

"Does he know you're coming?"

"He gave us his card," Grin answered, waving the slip of paper.

"One moment," she said slowly, rising from her seat and walking into an adjoining room. I looked around the office, clean and well lit, with a window facing the street. Compared to the Joseph Luby tailor shop, it was a palace.

Walter Trough, a robust and overweight old man with a bald head, emerged from the room followed by his secretary.

"I do not know these children!" he said with a scowl.

"Wait, we want to hire ya, and we can pay!" Grin shot back before we were whisked from the room.

The large man snorted. "Come in here."

Grin and I entered the small room and took a seat on a large leather sofa. Walter Trough remained standing behind a dark wooden desk.

"I don't do charity work."

"I saw your name in the paper, that ya helped those baseball players pro bono. I don't know much, but I know that means free."

"Famous men aren't charity—two very different things."

"Well, you're the kind of guy who likes his name in the paper, and I can get it in the paper."

Walter, intrigued, sat down.

"Hear us out. Tell him, Elsie." Grin turned to me.

"Well..." I said softly.

"Speak up, child. I cannot hear you."

"My father has been arrested."

"For what?" he said causally.

"For murder. I swear he didn't do it."

The old man leaned over the table. "Is he an immigrant?"

"Yes, we are German. But he doesn't speak English well, and that's the problem. I'm afraid they will put him away forever even though he is innocent!"

The old man shook his head. "He needs a good lawyer."

Grin shot up. "So you will help us?"

"For three hundred dollars."

I was struck speechless. "That is my father's whole year salary at the train yards."

"Three hundred dollars is what I cost. Like I said, I don't do charity work."

Grin was furious as he sprang to his feet. "She needs your help. He could die in the Tombs, and you know it!"

"I am the same price as every good, honest lawyer in this city. You will have to pay to free your father, young child. This is America."

Grin clenched his fists. Fearing he would do something unforgivable, I pulled him out of the office.

"Did you see the way he spoke at us? I could gather a hundred newsies who would pitch in three dollars. In a heartbeat!" he shouted, slamming the door to the elevator closed.

"It's alright. We'll find a way."

"That's it!" Grin's eyes lit up.

"What?"

"We'll collect a fund."

"But the strike."

"The strike will be over in a couple of days, I'm sure of it, and with the decrease to five cents a ten, I know we could do it. Ya in the brotherhood now. They would do it."

I threw my arms around him, ecstatic at a restoration of hope. Realizing I was clinging to Grin a little too tight, I pulled back, my face flushed red.

With the break of our embrace, Grin lowered his cap over his eyes. Even at his attempt to disguise it, I could tell that he too was blushing.

The elevator hit the ground floor, and we both rushed out of the elevator, putting some space between us.

To Grin's surprise, and mine, there was no movement on the end of Pulitzer and Hearst toward resolving the strike. Communication was coming though the circulation office managers, who only relayed false information at times to trick the boys into buying papers. At one point they said papers were now three for a cent, then five for a cent, then free! Kid, insisting that the committee needed to go directly to the editor of the *Journal* himself, gathered a group to descend upon the Park Row office.

Grin and I joined in and marched up and down the sidewalk with banners. We even sang songs of our plight.

My favorite was to the tune of an Irish song, "Annie Lisle," made up by the Irish boys of Bowery. The newsies added their lyrics with the usual flair:

Help the newsboys in their struggle
For our cause is just.
Don't buy the New York World *or* Journal.
Won't you please help us.
We will fight for our rights. We ain't no millionaire.
We newsies standing up for justice. We deserve our share!

To all the boys' delight, the lesser-circulated papers of New York, the *Sun* and the *Times*, the *Tribune*, the *Herald*, and even the *Brooklyn Eagle* approached the gathering to report on our demands. The boys loved finding their names in the editions, many of them calling themselves the "leaders of the strike" and citing themselves as the "one who started the whole thing." The reporters lapped up all the colorful stories the boys shared with them and took them as fact, even if they were flat out lies.

Finally, after an hour of waiting and chanting outside the *New York Journal* offices, a shiny black horse-drawn cab pulled up in front of the main door.

Kid leapt forward. "If that's Hearst, we should send someone to talk to 'im."

"Send Indian. He's the youngest," Dave said.

Blink looked over at Indian, "Go up an' ask 'im."

The boy's eyes went wide, and he hurried up to the door. As it opened, a tall man with a young, clean-shaven face, his hair parted in the middle and cut short, stepped out of the cab with a majestic stride.

The strikers fell silent.

"Are youse Mr. Hearst?" Indian asked.

Hearst stopped in his tracks and looked at the eager boy. His eyes then drifted up at the fifty of us with our banners and badges.

"Yes."

"We're the strikers, Mr. Hearst," Indian said in a sweet high voice.

Hearst bellowed low in what seemed like a laugh. Within a minute, another man stepped out of the cab and was at his side. He took Indian by the shoulder to usher him away when Hearst stopped him with a raise of his hand.

"Well, boys, what can I do for you?"

Kid Blink stepped forward, taking over. "We want one hundred papers for fifty cents."

Hearst looked to the man at his side. "Send up four boys."

I looked to Grin, who was just as surprised and awestruck as I was.

Hearst strutted into the building, and his assistant looked at Kid. With disdain and impatience in his voice, he spat, "You heard him. Only four of you boys. Which ones will it be?"

Kid and Dave decided to take a trusted man each. Kid chose Grin, and Dave took Scabooch.

I turned to Grin in surprise, but he was calm. The four boys continued into the building of the paper and left the world in which they belonged outside.

All was calm for ten minutes, the longest time I had ever seen the newsies go without talking. You would have thought God himself had struck them dumb. I considered walking over to the hot dog cart when Fitz shot up from his seat.

"De whole strike committee should be up there negotiatin'," rumbled Fitz.

A couple newsboys nodded. Monix, who had looked like he was merely in deep thought, shifted his weight to his knees and tipped his cap up. "They might be up there offerin' our boys bribes."

"Bribes? Can they do that?" spat one newsie.

"They can do anythin'," Monix said, leaning back and covering his face with his cap to take a nap. But the newsies weren't as calm as Monix. I could tell Fitz was starting to gather some steam.

I began to worry that if Hearst was offering Grin a bribe, he might accept the money for the lawyer. The last thing I wanted was Grin betraying his brotherhood because of me.

The minutes ticked by, and the boys continued to mumble rumors. I listened in for Grin's sake. However, twenty minutes later, the four boys exited the building with little flair or pomp.

"What'd he say?" the newsies said in unison, almost sounding like a chorus.

Kid emerged proudly. "He said he would give us an answer on Monday. I think we might 'ave won, boys!"

The boys cheered enthusiastically. Kid went on to recount step by step the details of the meeting.

"The lobby was real nice," Kid described. "Marble and crafted wood and stuff. We were led to his office and told to wait outside."

"It was about five minutes waitin'," added Dave.

"Then what?" they probed.

"We told him again what we wanted." Kid stood up. "I want one hundred papers for fifty cents, and so do all the boys of Manhattan, Brooklyn, and Long Island, and we're not backing down till we get it."

"What'd he say?" the boys echoed one another in expectation.

"The old man stroked his beard, stared us down, and said, 'I'll have to talk it over with some guys before giving an answer.' I then asked if we could arbitrate with 'em like he does with his own pape. He laughed and said if he needed to arbitrate, he'd meet us at the Broadway Central Hotel. Then, he added, he'd give us an answer on Monday," Kid finished, incredibly pleased with himself.

The fifty or so boys who were there were greatly encouraged. Attacks on the scabs became less of a priority, and the strike committee treated themselves to a nice meal.

Later that evening, while the boys were crowded around a table in the ally playing jacks and cards, Kid Blink, Grin, and Dave decided to huddle in a corner. Some of the boys didn't like this, and even brought up whether the boys' account of what happened with Hearst was truthful. Up until that point, it never occurred to anyone that they might have lied.

"I ain't likin' it. I think Hearst paid them off. Watch, they'll abandon us. You'll see," I overheard Fitz say low to Mikey.

I knew the boys couldn't care less about what I had to say, but I listened and grew angry at what I heard.

"Grin and Kid know something more, and they ain't sharin'." Fitz squirmed.

Later that evening, all the boys broke up and scattered to the four corners of Manhattan to meet with more strikers. I was quiet as I walked back to the church with Grin.

"So what really happened?" I asked Grin.

"What do you mean?"

"In Hearst's office. Quite an exciting place, but you all were very casual about the whole affair."

"The whole affair? There's no affair. Kid said the whole thing," Grin snorted, which really sent me into a fit.

I stomped my heels. "Then we aren't friends, " I shouted, "and we never were."

I took off in a huff. Grin let out a sigh and picked up his pace to catch me at the church gate.

"I don't know if I can trust you!" I snapped at him.

"I've given ya no reason not to. Why would you say that?"

"I don't know anything about you, Grin—why you won't go above Fiftieth Street, why you and Kid have this understanding, and why you feel you owe him something?"

Grin took a deep breath. "Is that what this is about?"

"Oh, and the book in back of your trousers, what is that for?"

Grin walked toward me. I grimaced back, feeling like he meant to yell at me or storm off, but he merely grabbed my hand.

"Come with me."

I pulled back.

"If ya want to know, then come on," he said, yanking my arm.

I didn't know what to think as Grin led me up Broadway, like we normally go when heading to the theaters. But as we approached 50th Street, Grin, to my amazement, kept walking.

"It's almost midnight. If the cops see us, we'll be picked up."

"Then ya better start movin' faster."

Chapter X

Hank Grinnan

At 54th Street, Grin took a hard left and ducked into an alley that sprouted off of 10th Avenue.

Eventually he stopped under the fire escape of a tenement and stared up at it ominously, like it was the gateway to a dark place.

"This was my home."

"Here?"

Grin shushed me. "They'll hear you."

"They?"

"My ma, my three sisters…and my pa."

"People say you're an orphan."

"I never say it. I don't lie, but I guess people think it from the way I talk."

"Why did you leave?"

"My pa liked his whiskey. Ever since I was six, he had me work odd jobs to make some extra money for it. I thought I was in some way helpin' my family. But it got to the point that it didn't matter if I brought home a good pay or not—he would beat me and kick me around. Worst of all, it got to the point where he wanted me to steal. Can you believe it—a cop askin' his son to steal wood from the yards? I knew it was wrong, and I didn't want to do it. One day I was caught, by the cop from the Tombs—rememba him?"

"Yes," I said, breathlessly hanging on Grin's every word.

"He saw who my pa was, and when he came to pick me up, he could sense somethin' wasn't natural. I confided in him, and he said he would help me out if I needed it. He knew very well what kind of man my pa was. So, one day I couldn't take the whippin' anymore, and I left. I found the church ya sleep in now and stayed there for a while."

"That explains a lot."

"One day I was out sellin' papes, and the boys wanted to go north up to Central Park. I went, thinkin' nothing of it. Well, my pa worked that section and saw me. He grabbed me by the neck, threw me down, and gave me the worst beatin' of my life. Kid saw this and lunged at my pa. He got in the midst of it, and my pa's horse kicked him in the eye.

"Kid was arrested, but he stood by me. He spat right back in the judge's face and said, 'If you ain't believin' me story that this boy was bein' knocked senseless by his pa in broad daylight for no good reason, then youse ain't no fair judge.'"

"He said that?"

"Yep, he served time for me, and we didn't even know each other all that well then."

"So that's the reason for his blind eye?"

"Yeah. When he got out, I was waitin' for him, said I would do anythin' for him. Besides, I felt guilty about his eye an' all. Kid got me out of the church and into the St. Vincent's Newsboy Home, showed me how to hawk papes better and how to work all the streets lower than 50th."

Grin got up from the crates and adjusted his cap, "Well, Elsie, that's my story."

"Thanks for telling me. But," I drew in a breath, "you passed Fiftieth. You said you never would."

"I pass Fiftieth once every week."

"Why?"

Grin pulled out a roll of dollars from his pocket. "I still take care of my sisters and my mother. My pa just doesn't know. He's too drunk most of the time to realize if Sarah has new shoes or there's bacon for breakfast."

Grin started to climb the fire escape. "Ya can come up, just have to be really quiet."

"Are you sure?"

Grin nodded. He was serious and intent on his delivery, a side of him I had never seen. As we approached the third floor of the apartment building, I noticed the window was cracked open, expecting his arrival.

"They know you come?"

"Just my ma."

Grin slid the window up a little more, being careful not to make a noise. He turned to me and said, "Wait here."

I watched in fear as Grin tiptoed into the apartment. I could hear snoring coming from inside. I took a closer look and realized that the room's two beds were not far from the window, one bed for his father and mother, and the other for his three sisters.

Suddenly the snoring stopped and my heart jumped. His father rustled in his bed.

Grin paused and then continued to creep toward an apron that hung on a peg a few feet from the window. But just as he was about to slip the roll of dollars in the pocket, a voice roared from the darkness.

"Who's there?"

Grin dropped the money securely into the pocket and without caution dove toward the window.

"Hey you! Sylvia, there's a break-in! Sylvia!"

Grin rolled down the fire escape in a hurry. I was already on the stairs.

"Hurry!" he cried.

Grin and I ran out of the alley and around the corner. Faint voices could still be heard above.

"Did they take anything, those snatches! Where's my gun?"

Grin leaned up against the wall, breathing heavily.

"I take it that's never happened before?"

He shook his head, too shook up to speak.

"Do you think your mother will be okay? Will he find the money?"

"Nah," he managed. "He didn't see me, I don't think. Come on, we should get back before anyone sees us."

I followed Grin, for the first time seeing fear in his eyes. His feelings for his father were so different from mine. Grin shuddered at the idea of his pa seeing him while I longed for just mere seconds with mine. In some way, I thought, this could have been much of the reason Grin wanted to fight to reunite me with Papa. We shared something he'd never had.

"Hank Grinnan, huh?" I brought up, once we were a safe distance away.

"What?"

"Your name…that you told my Pa."

"Yeah. Hank, short for Henry."

"I thought Grin stood for something else, you know…?"

"Stood for what?" He smiled, prodding me on.

"You know."

"Nah, I don't." He stopped, facing me.

"Your smile," I said low, blushing.

"What about my smile?" He grinned.

"Well, it's just, you know…nice I guess."

Grin laughed. "Ya like my smile?"

"No, it's just…" Too embarrassed to speak, I gave up and continued walking. "So I know everything about you now?"

"Everything," Grin stated flatly.

"No," I protested.

Grin stopped.

I pointed to his back. "The book in the back of your trousers."

"Oh," Grin chuckled, "not everything."

"And you're not going to say anything?"

Grin shook his head.

"Ah!" I threw up my hands, exasperated.

"But now *I* know something," he teased.

"What?"

"You like my smile."

And without one more word, he set out down Broadway, his eyes alert to dodge the late-night Metropolitan Police.

Chapter XI

Irving Hall

Sunday was a quiet day, mostly because there were no evening papers sold on Sunday, hence nothing to boycott. The boys took this as their day to strategize, plan a parade, and secure New Irving Hall to hold a rally. Word came through the ranks that important New York officials were now lending their support, including Timothy "Dry Dollar" Sullivan, a former newsie himself and now a state senator. Part of me wondered if this was another contact of Grin's, but he would never admit it.

This was also the day that the *World* and *Journal* decided they needed more scabs on their side and sent notices to the lodging houses "for bums," as Grin called them. They offered two dollars a day and the papes at forty cents a hundred. I wondered if, with all the incentives the papers were offering, it would have been cheaper to comply with the newsboys' demands. The goal of the papers was to keep them on the street at all costs, and the newsies were happy to make them pay.

As the strike committee went to all the papers with news of the mass meeting and their support from T.D. Sullivan, Grin and I set off with "newsie support" circulars to pass out around Downtown.

"I'm afraid the strike is gonna get more violent. I saw some boys with dynamite," Grin whispered to me as he passed out a circular and the man donated a penny to the cause in return.

"You don't think they would really use it, do you?"

"You never know. The trolley strikers do. As much as Kid wants to believe that the strike committee and the union mean somethin', it still doesn't hold weight with the boys. They're all their own businessmen, ya know?"

"I see what you mean."

"Boys are also gettin' impatient, starting to blame the leaders just to blame somebody."

"Kid?"

"Yeah, Kid and Dave mostly. They're easy targets."

"But Hearst said he'd give an answer tomorrow. That has to mean something."

"I hope."

Grin and I raised a dollar and a quarter by the time we were finished distributing the circulars. I enjoyed the lazy Sunday with Grin so much that I wondered what the past week would have looked like had there not been a strike.

Grin's forewarnings were correct. The next morning, the mass meeting was one of the most violent of the strike. In fact, the boys had kicked it off the night before by succeeding in tipping over a delivery wagon and seriously injuring the driver.

At 42nd and Vanderbilt, one hundred strikers fought two wagons and thirty men and big boys. They vigorously ripped up the papers in a flurry like a snowstorm, but not without a few bloody noses and thrown stones. On 125th and 3rd Avenue, three hundred strikers advanced across town and eventually up to the Harlem news offices, leaving a wake of attacks in the their path. If any "two-dollar" bums had decided to take the papers up on their offer, they were sure regretting it.

Grin wasn't happy with the news and informed Kid that the increase in violence only weakened the legitimacy of the union and gave Hearst reason not to take the boys seriously. "Ya can reduce the circulation and make an impact without the mass violence," Grin stressed. "It's different swipin' papes from a scab. Throwin' stones and clubs at the wagon drivers makes us look bad."

It didn't help the riotous and restless newsboys that the parade Kid promised never happened. After various excuses, Kid again insisted he would secure a permit from the mayor and the parade would happen the following day.

For the boys who needed ammunition to doubt their leaders, Kid failing on his promise to secure a permit for a parade that morning added fuel to their fire.

As the meeting at Irving Hall on Broome Street came to order, the crowd of united newsboys cheered so loud that those in the box seats felt a small earthquake. I joined in, getting up on my seat and shouting at the top of my lungs. I laughed to myself, thinking about how I could have been in the asylum, retiring to bed after an hour of silence. My "ladylike" manners had now morphed into spitting on a perfectly clean theater floor, muffling profanity under my lungs, and shouting so much that my voice stripped itself of its tender high quality, taking on a low, rough tone.

"Strike! Strike! Strike!" the crowd chanted in unison.

It wasn't even the interior that was rumbling with voices. The theater could only fit two thousand, so the extra three thousand supporters spilled out onto the street. Various delegations from Jersey City, Brooklyn, Harlem, Midtown, and Downtown were all represented.

My toes curled inside of my boots with excitement. This moment was mine as well. I tried to absorb the energy, the boys' spirit. This was a weapon I could use throughout my life, in all my battles."

Ironically, the featured speakers of the night had something else to fight for. On the stage, off to the side, was a big floral horseshoe donated by the *Brooklyn Eagle* to be given to the newsboy with the best speech. I could see various boys, including Grin, eyeing it throughout the night.

Mush, who introduced himself to the crowd as "Nick Myers," was elected chairman of the strike committee and the organizer of the night. He struggled for fifteen minutes to calm the boys. Finally, the boys settled to a low rumble, and Mush was able to introduce some of the prominent people of the crowd who had come to grant the boys well wishes.

L.A. Snitkin, a representative for Assemblyman "Charley" Adler, was the first to speak. "Mr. Adler is with you boys heart and soul, and he sends you best wishes. You've made a firm stand, boys, and have made a better showing than the motormen either here or in Brooklyn."

The next to speak was Frank P. Wood, introduced as the "Well, well!" man of the baseball field.

"Hooray for the strike!" he began. "You boys have been successful so far, and you must stick it out to the end. What right have these fellows got to hold out ten cents on you? Not a bit, and don't you stand for it. Keep the law, boys, and don't let me hear you using any dynamite. You can win peacefully. Just try it and see."

Phillip Wissig, an ex-assemblyman, got up and swaggered to the front of the crowd to recount his story. "I sold papers back in eighteen sixty, and I am proud of you for showing the spirit you did in fighting for your rights. You are only the rising generation, and if the older ones can't support you, they can at least treat you fairly. Now keep up the fight. Don't violate the law and don't use dynamite, but stick together and you will win."

Mush then called the last of the men to speak, Mr. Brennan, "the oldest war horse in the business."

"You have the sympathy of the News Dealers Association, and I expect the association will take action looking to your assistance, and we might have a public meeting tonight," the old man concluded.

Grin and Kid nodded to one another, proud that this latest support would be the key to their success.

Mush then turned the stage over to Dave, "the official president," he added. Without much pomp and circumstance, Dave came forward to read a set of resolutions, calling upon other news dealers and advertisers to assist the boys in their strike.

Suddenly I heard a boy behind me yell, "Traitor! You makin' a deal with Hearst." After this, there was an uproar among some of the boys. It was clear the Dave didn't hear what was said as he continued with his resolutions.

I looked to Grin who looked to Kid. Dave kept his face down, eyes low as he finished his speech. The boys behind me continued to razz him even after he took his seat.

Mush came to the stage and called for order. "Don't forget that this gentleman is the president of the Newsboys Union," he stressed.

The boy behind me snickered, "Not for long."

Next, Mush opened up the meeting to any newsboy who wanted to speak. The floral horseshoe stood proudly next to the podium, tempting their tongues to be next.

Racetrack Higgins immediately got up to speak. He looked like the kind who never backed down from an opportunity to shine. He was better dressed than the other newsboys, his boots were shiny, and he worked the crowd like a circus master as he recounted his latest tale of trying to obtain a permit for the strikers.

"Friends, ladies, and fellow strikers, I had gone to the chief of police meself for a permit for the parade with band music. Mr. Devery says to me, 'Go 'way, you slob,' and I says, 'Mr. Devery, don't call me a slob. I'm trying to make my living. I ain't so high up in office as you, but some day I may be *higher.*"

The theater rumbled with laughter. All the boys cheered and yelled their agreement with Racetrack. Loving it, Racetrack danced around the stage in his shiny boots, and the boys cheered on louder.

Indian hopped up next and quickly told the story he spread around all day. "I was told Mr. Hearst couldn't afford to sell the paper for less, says 'You see, he loses a hundred thousand a year.'"

The boys booed and got out of control before Indian could finish his speech. Reluctantly, once more, Mush got up to keep order.

"Boys, boys!" he spouted. They slowly trickled to a calm.

Before taking his seat, Mush glanced down to the newspaper reporters in the front row. "Oh, and please refrain from quoting these boys in a bad light, as saying 'dese' and 'dose' and 'youse'."

Indian popped up next to Mush "'Cause if youse dose, we'll soak ya!"

The boys exploded in laugher, riled back up. Mush threw up his hands and sat down.

When Kid Blink got up to speak, it was clear that many of the boys valued him over Dave. Some even cheered, "Our Master Workman!"

Before the meeting, I had heard Grin and Kid talking about what they would say to the boys and how important it was to settle down the fighting now that they had met with Hearst. "We're gonna do this the right way," Kid agreed with Grin, "through negotiation."

Kid cleared his throat before the crowd. "I don't agree with youse boys about goin' up and takin' papes away from people. What we wants is to stick together and not sell the *Journal* and *World*."

"You got it, Kid!" shouted boys in the crowd.

"Is ten cents in the dollar as much to us as it is to Mr. Hearst, de millionaire? Is it, boys?"

"No!" we shouted.

"We can do more with ten cents than he can with twenty-five. Am I right, boys?"

"Youse right!"

"I don't believe in hittin' the drivers of the news wagons. I don't believe in dumpin' the carts, same as was done in Madison Street last night. I'll tell you the truth. I was one of the boys that did it, but it ain't right. Just stick together, and we'll win. If we did it in 'ninety-three, we can do it in 'ninety-nine!"

"Yeah!"

"Now, you all know me, boys, don't you?"

"We do! We do!"

"Well, we'll all go out tomorra and stick together, and we'll win in a walk! We'll win it before Dewey comes home!"

In an instant, the boys were on their feet, shouting cheers. I stood up too. I wanted to spot Dave to see his reaction, but I couldn't see past the swarm of boys whooping and hollering for Kid.

Finally, it came time for Grin to speak. He put his hands in his pockets and shifted his weight onto his right leg, eyes shining bright against the lights of the stage. He eventually shushed them with his hand, which he immediately put back in his pocket.

"I'm not gonna lie. A man attempted to bribe me with two dollars to sell the yellas." The boys booed and hissed. I was surprised. Grin had never mentioned this to me.

"But I said I wouldn't take it because the man refused to contract to pay my hospital expenses."

The boys doubled over in laugher. Grin, unable to maintain a straight face, gave in too.

I loved seeing Grin up there in all his glory. His tall shape and unmatched confidence made him appear smarter and more important than the other boys who were on the strike committee. I remembered asking him why he never attempted to join the committee. "I work better from the shadows," he had said, "until I got somethin' to say."

Suddenly I noticed that Grin was looking at me, waving at me to join him.

"Nickel! Come on up!"

I balked, but soon all the Vincent boys were chanting "Nickel."

I caught my breath. It took me a while to understand that it wasn't just the Vincents, but that many others were cheering me on to speak.

Next thing I knew, I was thrust up on the stage, Grin ushering me into the center. "What do I say?" I whispered.

"Anythin' ya want."

"Well…" I said, trying to hear my own words amid the noise of the crowd.

"Hey," Grin shouted at Mikey, who was still yelling my name. "Hey there, Mikey, shut up, will ya?"

The room quieted. I took a deep breath. I'd never spoken in front of a crowd before. It was against everything in my nature. Finally, I managed to put on a bold look. "All I can say, boys, is to stick together and we'll win."

The boys clapped sporadically. I heard Mikey mumble, "Well, what do ya expect…she's a girl."

Fire rushed up inside me.

"Well, as a girl," I said pointedly to Mikey but loud enough for the crowd to hear, "I'm seeing what you boys are doing to each other. You don't listen, you spread rumors of bribes, and you change your allegiances depending on who's in the room."

The hall fell silent.

"Yes, some of these boys are real good at speaking, and they are speaking for you, so don't tear them down. When they say, 'Stick together,' they aren't saying it just to keep themselves as your leaders. They're saying that because they know the second you break apart with your lies and rumors, people are going to get hurt. And Hearst and Pulitzer win."

I felt dizzy and happy, right to my bones. I took a deep breath and held it. The boys' reaction was quick and mixed. Some leapt to their feet with cheers, others sank in their seats. Grin was flabbergasted. It was a sight I would never forget.

"That's all I've got to say to you." I curtsied. The boys loved it.

The horseshoe went to Kid that night as a top prize for his eloquent speech. I wasn't jealous. I was curious to know if Grin was, but I couldn't find him among the outpouring of newsies from the theater.

Eventually Racetrack grabbed my hand and ushered me to the Vincents, where they offered their congratulations for a great speech in their typical rough manner. In doing so, however, they attracted the attention of an officer who quickly approached and pulled them off of me.

"Sir, I'm fine. These are my friends."

"Miss, you will have to come with me."

A lump rose in my throat.

Racetrack rushed to my side. "She's my sista', offica'. She's me responsibility."

The officer eyed the boy. "You better take care of her. You boys were a little too rough for my liking."

"Soytenly, offica'."

The cop peeled away. Racetrack took me to his side protectively.

"Let's get youse outta 'ere," Racetrack insisted.

I nodded my head and joined the boys as they headed onto the main avenue. But before Irving Hall was completely out of sight, I took one last look around. By now, most of the boys had left, and there were only reporters and glory-seeking newsies milling about the front steps. It was no surprise that there was no sign of Grin.

Chapter XII

Betrayal

The next morning, I waited inside the attic for Grin, who was unusually late. I soon became solemn in my quietude like the praying parishioners in the church below. Alone with my thoughts in the hushed daybreak, I reflected soberly about all I'd done.

My mind drifted to the night before. I felt a fleeting sense of pride at the newsies' response to my speech. Having been the only girl to speak that night, I received some of the loudest cheers and applause. And then I realized, with a pang of guilt, that with the attention of one of the largest crowds I had ever witnessed, I made no mention of my father.

Surely, those men who cared about the injustice of the newsie would have cared that my father was wrongly imprisoned. Tears streamed down my face, and my heart pounded. I muffled my cries in my blanket. I knew I would never get that chance again.

I took a deep breath. I couldn't sit here alone waiting for Grin. I had to do something.

Fleeing the church with desperation, I walked and walked. I wasn't sure where to go or where Grin was. I tried making my way to Park Row for the parade, but every time I got within sight, I turned my heels and walked down another side street.

My thoughts raced. Grin was a good friend, maybe even more than a friend. I didn't know how to describe my feelings for Grin. But no matter how wonderful he was, no matter how much the newsies accepted me into the brotherhood, Grin wasn't my father, and the newsies weren't my family.

The only thing that finally stopped me in my tracks was a loud growl from my stomach. Looking up at the clock above City Hall, I saw that it was long past morning, and I was starving.

Giving in, I finally made my way toward the gathered crowd of newsboys on Park Row and was taken aback by what I saw.

The newsboys had not only succeeded in confiscating and shredding the papers from scabs and wagons but had also stormed the counting rooms and pulled the stacks from them, creating a blizzard of paper that formed six-inch snowdrifts along the street.

"Nickel!"

I turned my head in the direction of the voice, expecting to see Grin standing there towering over the smaller newsboys and tipping his hat. But it was a short, stocky Irish boy, someone I didn't recognize.

"Boys!" he said, motioning his friends. "It's the girl from last night."

The boys immediately collected around me, patting my back, shaking my hand. I tried to get out of the huddle, pulling and pushing my way out. Luckily, I spotted some Vincents.

"Mikey!" I screamed, running toward him. He turned and he looked pale.

"What happened to the parade?"

"Kid never showed. There was no permit, again. They think he's been lyin'. Then Dave showed up and stepped down as president."

"Where's Grin?"

Mikey shook his head, "Can't say nothin' right now." He dropped his voice low to a whisper.

Before I could ask why, Morris Cohen approached Mikey with five boys flanking his side. "Where are they, Mikey?"

"Don't know what youse talkin' about." He shook his head, faking a false bravado.

"I heard about Dave, and now Kid ain't here either."

Morris glared at me. "You know somethin?"

"Mikey, if you know something, tell them," I encouraged.

"I don't know nothin'!" he shouted. "I'm headed over to Mitchell's."

"No you ain't!" Morris's crony held Mikey up by the neck.

Racetrack made his way through the crowd. I tried to get close to him, but some of the Morris boys blocked my way. Racetrack was sticking close to them, which I found unusual.

"Nickel, Kid ain't here. They say he's sellin' papes," Racetrack said.

"Why? He wouldn't do that. After last night?"

"Mikey knows," Racetrack said with a solemn tone.

Mikey now was grasping at his neck, and his face was starting to turn from his reddish-white complexion to a pale blue.

Morris smirked, "Tell us, Mikey, or we're gonna lick ya."

Mikey swallowed hard. He had no choice.

"Kid was gone all last night. He wasn't at Vincent's. That's all I know."

The boy released Mikey and punched him in the gut.

"Hey!" I shouted, pulling Mikey to me, away from the boys. Racetrack stepped in and helped block the boys' path.

"Kid ain't no scab," Mikey shot back.

Something didn't add up. I started to worry as the boys carried on with violent banter. No one had a clear head, and it was difficult to tell what they were saying as their voices carried over one another, a myriad of "douse," "youse," and "sock 'em." As the boys got into a more heated conversation, I took the opportunity to grab Mikey by the shoulder and pull him off to the side.

"Where's Grin? You can trust me."

Mikey looked at the ground. "I dunno. Last night I saw Kid get picked up in a real nice cab—that's what I saw. If I tell the boys, they'll think he's been convinced by Hearst and Pulitzer to turn on them. I went to go find Grin, and he wasn't in the room either…Though Grin sometimes sleeps other places, youse know."

"But something isn't right."

"And it gets worse," Mikey said so low under his breath that I almost didn't hear it.

"What?" I said, breathless.

"Fitz was gone this morning," Mikey muttered. "Then I heard the lodge manager say he got a call Fitz was in jail, arrested for blackmailin' Hearst."

Now I was certain that something had happened with the boys last night, and once I could find out what that was, I thought, I'd be able to find Grin.

"Come quick!" one of the boys shouted. "Hurry!"

Mikey and I ran after Racetrack, Morris, and the rest of the boys as they set off with purpose. The mob of nearly three hundred boys charged down Park Row chasing after someone. When the horde of angry boys stopped, the nucleus dispersed, and I saw their prey: Kid Blink. Two officers had snatched him from the crowd, the reason for the abrupt halt of the pursuit. Kid, hands up in surrender, was in one of the nicest suits I'd ever seen on a boy his age. This only fueled rumors and confirmed suspicions that he had been bought.

"He's a scab! Wese got a right to soak him!" shouted one of the bigger boys.

"Do you have a permit for this gathering?" questioned the officer to Kid.

"He ain't with us," howled one of the boys.

Kid was frightened, and as his terror rose, he turned to the policeman. "No, sir, I got no permit. Youse gonna take me in?"

"That's right, run like a scab," one of the boys shot back.

"Kid," I shouted. "Kid!"

But he didn't look back as the police carted him off. I figured the rumors were true. He had betrayed the newsboys and was looking for safety in mistakenly being arrested.

A sick feeling boiled in my stomach. Nothing seemed fair or right anymore. If both Kid and Fitz had betrayed the newsboys, then I was at a loss for what Grin had done.

The mob broke up, and the boys went their separate ways. The members of the strike committee who remained agreed, under the guidance of their self-elected new president Morris Cohen, to meet again and appoint new positions. I decided to head north and see if I could find Grin at one of his favorite spots. My secret hope was that he had just taken the day to himself, away from the chaos, innocent and oblivious to the unraveling that had just occurred.

Chapter XIII

Scab of Sheep Meadow

The farther I walked uptown, the quieter the world became, and I joyfully welcomed it. Before I knew it, I was standing at the entrance to Central Park, lush and inviting. The air in the shade was unusually cool, and I felt like sleeping under an oak tree and washing my memory of the last two weeks.

Determined to find the right tree, I ventured into the park toward Sheep Meadow, where sheep grazed in an open field. I stopped and remarked at the sight. The sheep were a gift to the park forty years earlier. It was odd how they feasted under the shadow of the city completely unfazed. They even had their own sheepfold.

To the right of the meadow there was a path, known as the Central Park loop, where a young newsgirl was standing by a green wooden bench. She relaxed with a stack of papers that were nearly half her height, a look of boredom etched on her face.

I made the mistake of smiling at her when suddenly she shouted back at me.

"Come here you! Come here!"

I looked behind me, but there was no one. Indeed, it was I to whom she was calling.

"Yeah, you!"

Her face scrunched up in confusion as she looked me over.

"Are youse a boy or girl?"

I had forgotten I was still dressed as a boy and was so dirty I doubted Pa would have recognized me.

"What's it to you?"

"I need you to watch my papes. But I only trust girls."

"Me?"

"Yeah, you don't see anyone else, do ya?"

"How do you know I won't run off with them?"

She looked at me funny then said, "You ain't a boy, that's why."

"Sure, I'll watch them," I shrugged.

As she handed them over, I took one look then dropped them all over the sidewalk like a hot poker.

"Ya crazy?" she shouted.

"They're the yellows!" I shouted back in disgust.

"Well, they ain't gonna bite ya," she sneered, picking them up.

"You're selling the yellows," I said in disbelief.

"So, what's it to ya? The *World* is the best pape to sell, especially with the strike. You can't find it anywhere."

"Exactly, the strike. Why…?"

"That's the boys' fight. We girls are different. Plus, they won't soak a lady."

"Just because they won't soak us doesn't give us the right to sell 'em."

"We're girls. We're different is all."

"No, we're not different. We all need to stick together to make the strike work."

The newsgirl was not convinced. After she stacked the papers, she set them beside me on the ground. "Well, you ain't got to touch them. Now I sure you won't run off with them. Look, there's a peddler on the corner over there that owes me two red hots, but he won't give them to a scab. He can't see me with the papes. I promise I'll bring you back one."

I relented. "Fine."

And with that the girl ran off.

I stood there staring at the papers in conflict. Every time crowds passed by, I froze, praying they would not ask for one. But no one in particular seemed to be walking close enough to the bench, and I began to evaluate that this newsgirl had not picked a very good spot. The most vital part of being a newsie is to know how to pick a good spot.

After a couple minutes, I considered leaving. However, even though this girl felt no loyalty to the strike, she was earning a living with these papers, and by abandoning her I knew I would be doing the wrong thing. So I stayed.

Then, as I had feared, a patron approached to buy a paper. I spotted her before she spoke. She was the most beautiful woman I had ever seen, tall and slender with an hourglass figure. Atop her slender neck was a small rounded face with crimson red lips, which complimented her golden brown hair swept up and piled high under a hat filled with white and pink flowers.

"Dear, you're a young girl!" she said, surprised, as she approached, her voice breathless, full of spunk yet still sophisticated. "Well, despite how you are dressed, I would like to buy one of your papers."

"Excuse me?" I was still so stunned by the sight of her I had forgotten the papers were by my side.

"That is the *World*, is it not?"

I glanced down. "It is, miss."

She smiled, her pursed lips parted in a playful manner.

"You seem shocked by this." The woman opened her coin purse. "Oh dear, I only have a five piece. Do you have change?"

"I don't, miss."

"Should I wait while you go get some?"

"No, miss," was all I could say.

At this she grew rather impatient. "I've searched the entire town for two hours looking for the *World*."

"Because of the strike," I explained. "There are no editions because the newsboys are on strike."

"Oh." She seemed caught off guard. "Then I will give you the five piece, and you may keep the change."

She held out the five piece for me to take. It seemed so shiny and gold, it would buy food for three days if I spent it right.

"I am sorry, I cannot."

Her soft eyes stared at me in confusion.

"First off, these are not my papers but belong to a girl who left for a moment. And second, I support the strike with every bone in my body and will not, even for a five piece, be a scab."

The woman's brow furrowed, and then to my surprise, she began to laugh. She laughed so hard that she eventually collapsed on the bench beside me.

"Do you mind if I ask what is so funny?"

The woman took a deep breath and then proceeded to take off her hat filled with flowers and place it beside her on the bench. She turned her sweet, inviting face to me and smiled. "My name is Isabelle Thornton. What is yours?"

"Elsie...Lutz."

"It's very nice to meet you, Elsie." She took another breath. "It has been a most exhausting day. You see, Elsie, in that paper there is a story about my father Alfred Thornton. Surely they are terrible and untrue things. However, although they be untrue, my family intends to ignore the allegations, so much so that they refuse to even find out how they are being reported in the *New York World*."

"I see."

"I took it upon myself to ignore my family's wishes of denial and seek out the paper myself. As I told you, it has taken me two hours to even find it, and my feet are very sore. And now that I have found you, you have given me every reason not to buy the paper."

"It is quite funny," I smirked.

"It is." Isabelle smiled. "But to find such a truthful young girl is not funny—it's refreshing."

"Thank you," I said humbly, under my breath.

"However, may I ask, if you are refusing to work, why aren't you in school or with your family?" she asked this with a very honest face. She was not at all like the Reformer, but I still resisted telling her anything.

"I'm afraid things were also said about my father that were terrible and untrue."

Her smile faded, and her eyes warmed with sympathy.

"I haven't many places that I can be, but to tell you the truth, Miss Thornton, I prefer this small piece of sidewalk right now to anywhere else."

"When is the last time you've eaten?" she asked with concern.

"Last night, before sundown."

"And far past noon today!" she said, surprised.

"You didn't run!" the newsgirl yelled as she ran back with only one red hot in her hand.

"Oh, 'ello, lady," the girl said, stopping in her tracks. "Come to buy a paper?"

"No thank you. I ended up not needing the paper."

"Sorry, they only had one red hot," the girl lied as she picked up her papers. "'Have a nice day," she said as she stuffed the red hot in her mouth and walked off to another part of the path.

"Young Elsie Lutz, I would like to give you a meal, if you have the time. What do you say?" Isabelle insisted.

"Well…you can't ask any questions, and I won't give you any answers," I spat, maybe a little too harshly.

She smiled. "Agreed. So, you will come?"

My stomach growled and I nodded.

Chapter XIV

The Gibson Girl

Isabelle Thornton was a perfect depiction of the Gibson Girl, illustrated in the popular magazine *Harper's* as a beautiful, young, spirited woman who was not only completely feminine but also independent. She wore the popular stiff shirtwaist and the big plumed hat. Her flowing skirt was hiked up in the back with a hint of a bustle.

Her townhome wasn't far from the east side of Central Park and was magnificent, a towering three-story house with a white façade and pillars that framed the doorway. The paved stoned street was the complete opposite of Orchard Street. It was pristine, there were no children playing outside, and it was so quiet that you could actually hear a bird chirp.

We entered the foyer. Isabelle whisked her hat off and threw the "dreadful heavy thing" on a neighboring table. She started to move off to the kitchen when she realized that I stood dead in my tracks staring at the brilliance of the furnishings before me. The most elaborate was a four-foot oil painting above the fireplace.

"That is a portrait of my family," she hinted in the direction of my stare.

I had assumed as much. It depicted the towering figure of her father on the right, standing behind three seated girls, one of whom I believed was her mother. Two proud strapping men stood behind the ladies on the left. A small white dog sat at the feet of the women. Underneath the portrait was the most elaborate mantelpiece for a fireplace I had ever seen, carved out of black marble.

"I'd give you a tour, but I am afraid you will faint before I finish showing off the parlor. I must give you food. I must."

As we moved down the hall toward the kitchen, I caught sight of a beautiful bouquet of flowers under a glass dome.

"They're wax," Isabelle said casually as we passed.

Wax flowers, I thought. I was truly in a home of wealth.

"Abby!" she shouted as we entered the kitchen.

An Irish woman with the fairest skin and fiery red hair was wiping her hands with a towel as she turned.

"Oh, Miss Thornton, have you tired of bringing in enough stray animals off the street that you've switched to children?"

Isabelle laughed. I smirked.

"She is dreadfully hungry. Can you please prepare a meal?"

"Oh course, what would you like, my dear?"

I had never been asked what I wanted for supper.

"I dunno," I finally muttered.

"I have some lamb and potatoes."

"Thank you," I agreed.

"I just hope you can do something about all the poor girls on the street, Miss Thornton—put that degree to good use."

"Degree?" I asked, never hearing the word used before.

Abby chimed in, "A law degree. My sweet girl, you are looking at one of only four female lawyers in all New York. New York State, that is!"

"You're a lawyer!" I shouted. "How…?" I stumbled.

"Come here, I'll show you."

Abby continued to prepare my meal as Isabelle led me to the neighboring library filled with large thick leather-bound books. Isabelle illuminated a bronze gasolier as we entered the room.

"These are all my father's books and a few of my brothers'. I studied them all."

"You read all these?"

"Most of them. Against my father's will, I took the New York Bar."

"Your father didn't want you to do it?"

"He didn't think I could."

"I can't believe it…"

"I'm sure I will put it to good use one day. Illinois has made it lawful for a female to preside as a lawyer. However, no one, no woman, has challenged the New

York law in the Manhattan courts yet."

I watched as she perused the books with a tender hand. Thoughts raced through my mind, but only one tugged at me: the image of my father in his cell in the Tombs. It was then I knew I needed to trust Isabelle, for my father's sake.

"Miss Thornton?"

"Yes, Elsie?"

"My father is in jail."

Her brow furrowed. "Why?"

"They say he killed a man, but he didn't. I know he didn't."

"We're is he now?"

"He's in the Tombs awaiting his trial."

Tears streamed down my face. "My father is the best man I've ever known. When my mother passed, he worked so hard to care for me. And we did well. We were very happy."

I couldn't hold it in any more. The emotion poured out of me until the sobs were so loud they brought Abby in from the kitchen. Isabelle held me close and let me cry. After a moment I looked up at her.

"Would you help me? Can you help me?" I managed through the tears.

Her face stared down at me, and she smiled. "I was just waiting for you to ask."

Abby's dish of lamb and potatoes was so delicious, I had two servings. After my meal, Isabelle showed me to the room of her younger sister, who was away in Philadelphia with their mother for the week. I was given a change of clothes and shown the bathroom, where a fresh hot bath awaited me.

"I will be downstairs to welcome my aunt for tea, and then once you are clean and rested, we will talk more about your father."

"Thank you," I exhaled. It was all I could say.

It was a glorious feeling to have a hot bath, a steaming hot bath. I almost fell asleep. I couldn't believe I had been this lucky. Maybe Grin had brought me this luck by not showing up to greet me this morning, I thought. Maybe all the bad had happened so that I could have all the good.

Wrapping myself in a dry towel, I stepped out and glanced back down at the bath water in the porcelain claw-foot tub. Judging by its dingy color, it had been two or three weeks since I last bathed.

Hanging on a satin hanger on the glass knob of the bathroom door was Isabelle's sister's white linen and lace dress. I studied it like a fine work of art. It was perfectly pressed and beautiful, but there was still something about Fitz's hand-me-downs that I cherished.

As I slipped on my new clothes, I imagined that in that moment the newsboys were picking their new committee, Fitz was in some police station, and Kid was being arraigned by the magistrate for his disturbance. And although it hurt me that I didn't know what had happened to Grin, it hurt even more that he had not reached out in any way to send a message.

My thoughts were interrupted by noises echoing from the lower floor. Isabelle's aunt had arrived. I only needed to wait for her visit to end to see my father again.

I tiptoed down the stairs so as to not disturb Isabelle and her aunt's active discussion.

"No, Isabelle, that is not our responsibility," I heard her aunt say.

"Indeed, it is. It is my gift. It is what I was given by the Lord, to help children in this way. Not your way, but my own."

I knew pretty quickly that I was the topic of conversation, so I stopped and waited midway down the stairs.

"Your father, my brother-in-law, is in a deep terrible mess, and you wish to call more attention to him by finally coming forward to practice law?"

"It is not a terrible thing. It is an honorable thing, Aunt Sophie."

I descended the final steps with cause, hoping to put my two cents into the conversation, but I was stopped cold. My heart nearly fell out of my chest. Both faces turned my way: Isabelle...and the Reformer Sophia Dannon.

She was dressed in her usual black long-sleeved frock. Her eyes immediately recognized me, and she rose to her feet.

"I know this girl!"

I backed away instinctively, my heart beating so fast that I swore it might explode.

"No...no..." I shook my head.

"Dear girl!" she said accusatorily. "This girl is a runaway from the asylum."

I backed farther up the stairway as the Reformer edged closer, blocking me in. Isabelle stepped forward to stop her, but Miss Dannon was already up the stairs, reaching for my arm.

I didn't even have time to think. I flipped my body over the railing of the stairway and slid across the polished floor toward the door. Running with all my strength, I reached the foyer and lunged for the doorknob.

"Elsie!" Isabelle shouted.

"Come back here, child, now!" shouted the Reformer.

Breaking free, I took off down the street, panting and close to tears. I didn't know if my escape had been the right decision, but I had to do all I could to avoid going back to the asylum. I slowed down my pace as I fell out of sight of the Thornton home.

Doubt was flooding my brain. I wanted to return and trust that Isabelle would fight for me, but I continued walking. I felt even more lost when a reflection in a storefront window reminded me that I was dressed like a daughter of wealth in my white linen dress. Suddenly a whistle echoed in front of me.

I exhaled and braced for the only person in that moment who could be worse than the Reformer: Rat.

Chapter XV

The Tunnel

I figured one reason for Rat's name was his small and unexpressive eyes, like those of a sewer rat. Up close, they offered no mystery or insight into his soul.

"If I ain't been given a gift from 'eaven," Rat cackled.

Rat's cronies seized me, and I screamed for help. In a snap, Rat lifted his hand and struck me across the jaw, sending a stinging sensation through my mouth. My eyes filled with tears, anger, and hate. Grin was right. Rat would hit a girl.

"Grin will kill ya, Rat! He'll kill ya!" I shot back in retaliation.

"Don't youse worry. If I knows Grin, he'll come and get ya."

At this time, New York was building the Interborough Rapid Transit, a railway under the streets known as a "subway." Rat and his boys had found that these newly birthed tunnels would make the perfect playground.

The boys led me down a sewer to one of these underground tunnels that had been abandoned by the workers, probably for its instability. By the look of it, it was similar to the parts my father had told me about that suffered from cave-ins that injured many of the men he knew from the railroad.

The boys placed me in a corner, and Rat watched me like a hawk as he paced in deep thought. Finally, he turned to a large boy who looked just like the one Fitz had been arrested for punching. "Joe, go tell 'im, quick. We want four hundred, nothin' less."

Joe nodded and ran out.

"Why do you want me here?"

"'Cause of Grin."

"I don't know how you are even going to find him."

"Oh, we know where he is."

"They say he's a traitor now, a scab like you," I mumbled, trying to deter him.

Rat laughed. "Grin's much more than that." He leaned in close to me. "He's de man now. He's the one talkin' with Hearst."

"What?"

Rat rubbed his fingers together. "He's the one close to all the money. And now with you, I'll get my fair share, my piece of the pie."

"Grin doesn't have any money!" I shot back.

"You dunno how it works. Hearst's gonna make Grin a scab. Grin's worth at least four hundred to Hearst right now."

"How are you gonna do that?"

"With you. He can get you unharmed for four hundred."

I swallowed hard at the word "unharmed."

"He won't do it," I said, doing all that I could to convince him of how flawed his scheme was.

"Like I said, he's honorable. That's his weakness."

Rat smiled from ear to ear. His lips spread, revealing a few missing teeth, with the small ones that remained blackened and rotting. His breath reeked of rotten cheese.

In that dark and damp tunnel, I regretted my flight from Isabelle. I would happily have risked returning to the asylum rather than to have Grin become a scab.

As they waited for the large boy to return, Rat and his cronies played craps, lost their money, played more craps, and had the money circulate right back to its rightful owners once more. All this happened with fistfights and dirty words flying all around, in between every roll.

Time was irrelevant in the cold, dark tunnel. Whether it was late afternoon or midnight, I had no clue. I was stuck and at the mercy of Rat and his men. I figured if I was waiting for something, I was waiting for them to fall asleep and I would navigate my escape. Surprisingly, I wasn't fearful. I was a lot stronger than the Elsie my father knew.

Suddenly a noise rustled from the end of the tunnel. Rat looked up.

"Joe?"

There was no response.

Rat stood up and moved closer to the black, dimensionless tunnel. "Joe! Come out, you goon!" Rat's voice echoed.

"Eh! What's that?" One of the boys pointed ahead. But Rat's eyes were already fixed on it, a tiny red light that was growing bigger and bigger.

Some of the boys backed up, but Rat inched forward, perplexed by the tiny light.

"It's a sewer cat or somethin', probably got a collar on, just reflectin' sunlight," Rat smirked at the scared boys.

But the single light got bigger and brighter as if it was moving forward.

Then, through the darkness, the source of the light was revealed, the inflamed end of a lit stick of dynamite held by Grin.

"Dynamite!" screeched one of the boys.

"You crazy! I'm out of here," echoed a couple of the boys as they scrambled for the escape ladder. Rat held his ground.

"Do you have de money?"

"What does it look like? Elsie, come here," Grin signaled.

I got up, but the two largest boys who had stayed behind were on me immediately. "Do not release her," Rat instructed. "I ain't got my money yet."

"Then ya gonna be blown to pieces."

"And so is youse."

"That's the chance I'll take. But I'm in control of this wick, and I can pull it out if you set Elsie free."

Rat's stern bravado was faltering. He looked back at the boys for support, but they were just as clueless as he was.

The boys faced off, staring down one another to test each other's wills, like the cowboys in dime novels.

Suddenly, Rat lunged at the dynamite, throwing Grin to the ground. The two wrestled, scrapping at each other's faces, reaching for control of the wick.

"Stop it! It's gonna blow," yelled one of Rat's boys.

Rat reached for the wick, but Grin pulled it around to the other side, out of Rat's reach.

"Stop! Stop!" I yelled, seeing the dynamite was about to blow.

"I'm outta here!" The two boys ran off, leaving me with no captors.

"Grin!" I shouted to get his attention.

"Run!" Grin said. "Run!"

Without thinking, I started to run into the dark tunnel as fast as I could go when—*bang!*—the entire tunnel shook, and the loud explosion sent me falling to the ground.

For a moment, I blacked out, but I was shaken awake by pieces of chipped rock falling overhead.

I crawled through the darkness, back in the direction of the boys.

"Grin!"

There was no response. My eyes adjusted to the darkness, and I made out two unconscious figures, Grin and Rat.

"Grin!" I shook him, but he didn't wake. He was buried under fallen debris and was bleeding on the side of his face. I held him close, tears streaming down my face.

"No!" I cried, "Please, no!"

I couldn't feel him breathing. Quickly, I removed the debris bearing down on his stomach. In doing so, I saw his chest expand, letting in a large breath.

His right eye opened.

"Grin?"

He tried to give a soft smile, but it ended up as a cough. He stopped trying to speak and just exhaled. He parted his lips and whispered, "Hospital."

Chapter XVI

Winning

The hospital was one large room with wide wood floorboards and a dozen windows along each side that flooded "healthy" light into the space. A row of beds lined each wall, which allowed the nurses to keep an eye on all the patients at once.

Every bed was filled. I walked along, scanning each one for Grin, trying not to look too long for fear of what injuries I might accidentally see. Most of the patients were covered in bandages, while others were completely hidden under white sheets up to their shoulders.

Grin was about halfway down the hall. My heart sank at the sight. His left eye was swollen shut, burns lined the side of his face. His right arm was wrapped in a sling. I took a seat on the chair next to him.

In the silence, I went back and forth between staring out of the large window to view the street below and watching Grin as he slept.

"Elsie."

I turned. Grin's right eye was open. He struggled to smile.

"Don't move," I instructed him. "Do you hurt?"

"How do I look?"

"You look like you hurt."

He chuckled and then grimaced from the pain.

"You shouldn't have done what you did," I said softly.

"What would you have suggested I done?" Grin asked.

"I dunno."

"All the boys were gone. I needed to do something drastic that Rat would understand."

"A stick of dynamite?"

"I was plannin' to pull the wick."

"Why didn't you?"

"Rat pulled it from my hand and flung it, idiot. Where is he?"

Grin tried to sit up. I gently helped him.

"Is Rat here?"

I took a breath, then shook my head no. "Rat died."

Grin was silent.

"The police knew it was an accident," I explained. "They said they've had a lot of trouble with the boys in the tunnel and they are always trying to run them out of there. They figured Rat was playing with the dynamite when it went off."

Grin let out a sigh. "I'm glad you're okay."

"I would have been alright if you had met me at the church in the morning."

Grin had a look of shame. "All this was my fault."

"Where were you?"

Grin stroked the white sterile sheets of the bed.

"I saw Kid get in a nice cab supplied by Hearst last night, and I knew what they were gonna do, offer him six hundred dollars. At least that's what he told me later when I caught up with him."

"Six hundred dollars!"

"He said he didn't. But I'm not sure. While we were talkin', Fitz was furious and said it wasn't fair. He deserved money too, so he went over with Jack and Henry to see if he could get a cut. I went to try and stop them. When we entered the office, I was gonna talk with Hearst, but they set a trap to make it look like blackmail. I jumped out of the window, but the other boys weren't so lucky. Thing was, Kid was standin' right there."

"Kid didn't speak up for them?"

"Nah. So I was mad, and I went to go see Walter Trough."

"The lawyer? Oh, no, Grin, you didn't! You shouldn't have…not for me."

"Nah, Elsie, it's not what you think."

"You didn't hire him with bribe money?"

"Nah."

"Then why did you go?"

"It was clear that Hearst and Pulitzer were purposely avoiding the union, only talkin' through the circulation mangers to relay their offers. And I couldn't go to Hearst alone without it bein' viewed as extortion or being a traitor. So I got Walter Trough to come with me."

"The lawyer? Why?"

"Simple, he wanted a chance to meet Hearst. He's a bit of a fame seeker. Plus, he liked my argument."

Grin tried to sit up a little more. I helped position his arm across his body as he continued, charged to tell me the story.

"I figured that what the *World* and *Journal* was doing was illegal. Ya see, they priced six cents a ten during the war, like other papes did, to cover the cost of the extra editions, like a war tax. But the other papes dropped their prices back to five cents except the *World* and *Journal*. So the papers were enacting a tax on us that we couldn't pass on to the customer. Trough agreed with me that it was a strong argument. So we took it to Hearst."

"What happened?"

"Hearst offered fifty-five cents a hundred, and newsies could return papes at half price."

"You did it!"

"I found the boys in a meeting to elect a new committee and told the boys…but they rejected it."

"They said no?" I asked, stunned.

"What the committee doesn't understand is that the boys are gettin' restless. Hearst will continue to ignore the union and speak directly through the circulation managers. Especially with the incentives, I'm not sure how long the boys will hold on. I'm hopin' they can go to a compromise."

"Well, with Kid and Dave gone, a new committee, and now boys arrested for extortion, I'm not sure it's the same strike now." I sighed.

"I was worried when ya weren't at Park Row. I searched everywhere, then one of Rat's henchmen found me at Vincent's…"

I shook my head in shame.

"Why were you in Rat's territory and dressed like that?" He gestured to my white linen dress.

I told Grin about Isabelle, how I fled the moment I saw the Reformer, and how I had ruined my chances of freeing my father.

"Ya should go back," he said. "Ya *will* go back and tell her everything, and you'll free your father."

"But how can I now? What do I say?"

"Sometimes winnin' doesn't look the way we want it to. Ya should be strong, Elsie, with whatever happens to your Pa."

A tall doctor with a slick black handlebar mustache approached with a nurse carrying a wood box, which she set on the table.

The doctor opened it up and took out a small bottle of white powder. He dipped a tiny spoon into it and scooped up some of its contents. Empting it into a glass of water, the powder quickly dissolved.

"Drink this," he said, handing the glass to Grin. "It's a new drug called Aspirin, it will help with the pain."

Grin drank the entire glass and handed it back to the doctor.

"You suffered a lot of interior trauma, young man. It's a miracle you are sitting up talking."

I lowered my head, still feeling responsible.

"Your family should be here momentarily." The doctor concluded as the pair advanced to the next bed.

"Then I have to get you out of here," I resolved, "before your pa..."

Grin gabbed my arm to calm my hysteria.

"It's okay."

"No it's not! Your father will take you back..."

"I've already seen my pa."

"You have?"

A voice boomed from behind. "Henry." The man it belonged to was well over six feet with an overwhelming presence like a prizefighter. He approached Grin's bed.

"Hi, Pa." Grin swallowed. "This is Elsie."

Grin's father did not smile but nodded. "Nice to meet you, Elsie."

"My mother's ill with tuberculosis," Grin explained. "Her doctor says fresh, dry air is the only thing that will help her."

"I don't understand."

"We are moving to Kansas, and Henry's coming with us," Grin's father explained in a calm tone.

"They're movin' to a farm, Elsie." Grin smiled. "And they need me."

"No!" I demanded. "You can't make him. Can't you see he's hurt? He's worked hard to end the strike, and now he's almost done it. They need him!"

I looked down at Grin, but he didn't say a word.

"Grin?"

"I think it's time I went with them."

"No, you can't. I need you."

"Not anymore. You've found the help you need. Return to that lawyer and free your pa. Ya need to do it now or you'll lose him forever."

"Grin…"

Tears formed in my eyes. He reached over his broken arm under his pillow and pulled out the book that he kept in the back of his trousers.

"This is my journal."

"Your journal?" I smiled, the final mystery explained.

"I want ya to have it. I'll begin a new one out West."

I took the leather-bound journal and clutched it like a Bible into my chest.

"Won't I see you again?"

"I'll come back for ya. I'm gonna make some money, and then maybe ya can move out too, ya and your pa. I hear there's a lot of room out there." Grin winked.

Mr. Grinnan cleared his throat, visibly uncomfortable at the sign of my emotion. "I'm gonna go get your sisters," he mumbled as he walked away.

With no one around, Grin held my hand and continued, "My pa stopped drinking. He's been doin' everything to help my ma, workin' double to buy the medicine she needs. Maybe he hasn't changed as much as I want him to, but he's old now, and I have to be the one to take care of my family."

"I understand," I whispered, enjoying my hand in his.

"Ya have to go back to Isabelle, as soon as you can."

"I know."

"Elsie?"

I looked up, unable to stop the tears rolling down my face.

"Do ya remember how ya spoke up at the meetin' in Irving Hall?"

I nodded.

"You're stronger than ya think. You're not the same girl I tripped at Vanderbilt."

"Tripped? I fell. My shoes came undone…"

"I tripped ya." His face flushed red. "I thought…I dunno. I wanted a moment to talk to ya, so I did a stupid boy thing, and I tripped ya."

"So outside the asylum?"

"I knew ya were there. I knew it was ya when ya called down to me. Why would a newsie pick that spot?"

I laughed, "So this whole time?"

Grin nodded.

"Don't go," I whispered.

Grin clutched my hand tightly. "Remember what I said about winnin' not always lookin' the way we want it to? This is one of those times."

Grin and I sat there in silence, the opportunity of our lives as blank as a sheet of paper before us. All we were certain of was that we wouldn't write them together.

Chapter XVII

A New Voice

I inched toward the door of Isabelle's Upper East Side townhome with trepidation. In choosing to accept my fate of being returned to the asylum, I hoped that Isabelle would have sympathy and try to help my father in any way she could.

Before my trembling fist knocked on the door, it swung open. To my surprise, Isabelle stood before me, looking tired and worn. Without hesitation, she whisked me into her arms and held me close. "Where have you been? I've had everyone searching for you, all over the city."

She pulled me away to examine my state. "Are you alright? Are you hurt?"

I shook my head.

"Come in quick," she said, ushering me inside. "We haven't much time."

In the parlor sat two young gentlemen whom I immediately recognized from the portrait: Isabelle's brothers.

"These are my brothers, Richard and William," she rushed, not intent on a full introduction.

I looked past the parlor, expecting to see the Reformer appear from the shadows at any moment.

"You can relax," Isabelle explained. "My Aunt Sophia isn't here."

I exhaled. "She's not going to take me back to the asylum?"

"I cannot guarantee that. She is quite headstrong. But for now we have bigger problems."

"Problems?"

"I've visited your father twice."

"You have?"

William spoke up. "The trial is today."

"It's today?"

"Yes," Isabelle said, leading me to sit in the parlor. "They were all set to assign your father a public defender."

"Robert Farmer," laughed Richard. "A wretched man. He made a 'deal' that your father would only have to spend twenty years in prison if he plead guilty."

"Twenty years!"

"Do not worry, Elsie. Your father has agreed that I be his council." Isabelle smiled.

"But we can't offer you any money," I said.

"Needn't worry about that. It's as much a risk for your father to have Isabelle as his council," snorted her brother.

"Richard!" she corrected.

"Why?" I asked.

"It's my first case," Isabelle said through clenched teeth, waiting for my reaction.

"You will be wonderful." I smiled.

William stood up. "We have a lot to do. We need to make our way to the courthouse."

"I must change!" Isabelle exclaimed.

"Why? You look beautiful," I said, admiring her pink satin dress and pearls.

Isabelle ran out of the room. Her brother laughed again. "It's hard for women. They can't look too pronounced in the courtroom, yet they mustn't lose their femininity."

I was considering this when Isabelle returned in a long black dress with lace around her neck and cuffs. A gold brooch perched in the center of her lower neck. Fixing a simple black hat with a blue feather to her puffed-up hair, she refreshed her face with makeup.

"William, what do I do with the hat?"

"I don't know," he shrugged.

"We must go," Richard said, impatiently looking at his watch.

"It's inappropriate for a lady to be seen in public without her hat, and yet it offends the court for a lawyer to wear his hat while addressing the judge and jury."

"Isabelle." Richard stomped his foot.

I took Isabelle's hand. "You look beautiful with or without your hat, and you will be a great lawyer with or without your hat."

Isabelle's troubled look broke into a large smile, and she embraced me once more.

"Here I am worrying about my appearance, and you are suffering so much, yet you encourage me. I will do everything I can, Elsie, everything I possibly can."

In the courtroom, restless reporters had gathered on the rumor that a lady would be presiding as a criminal's representative in a murder trial. They were eager with their notepads and pencils to see if the judge would allow such an audacious thing. The prosecution representing the State of New York in accusing my father of murder was Herbert Smith, an older man of fifty, dressed in a pinstripe suit.

He repeatedly spat chewing tobacco into a spittoon positioned at his feet while staring at Isabelle in an unprofessional manner. I didn't know whether this was to unnerve her or if he simply could not pry his eyes away from her.

Richard and I were positioned at the back of the courtroom in the last row of seats. Isabelle did not want my presence to be known, but the distance combined with the high number of reporters made it virtually impossible to see my father.

"Order in the court!" Judge Quigley banged his gavel. "We are gathered here today to hear arguments in case 102-99, the State of New York versus Dietrich Lutz. Mr. Smith?" the Judge signaled.

After one more spit of tobacco, Mr. Smith stood to face the jury of twelve men.

"Mr. Chief Justice, may it please the court, the state of New York has the right to bring to trial, convict, and punish this man Dietrich Lutz for the murder of John Pyle on July fourteenth of this year eighteen ninety-nine."

"Who is the counsel for the defendant?"

Isabelle removed her hat and rose. "I am, Your Honor."

A rumble of chatter echoed through the courtroom.

"I am afraid, Miss…?"

"Thornton," she finished for the Judge.

"Miss Thornton, you shall seek different representation for this man."

"Can I not be his lawyer?"

"No, miss, this is my courtroom and it is my decision to see who is fit to practice law in my courtroom."

Isabelle held back her fury as she glanced down at her brother William.

"I am as fit as any man, Your Honor."

"This is not a trial for a woman lawyer. It is uncivil and unclean. Women are more suitable in office practice than in courtroom practice, especially in criminal cases."

I noticed the stenographer had stopped typing. She looked just as angry as Isabelle.

Isabelle sighed and looked to her brother, who then rose. "I will take over, Your Honor, if it pleases the court."

"No!" I yelled, jumping up onto my seat.

The reporters roared, and the judge banged his gavel. "Order in the court!"

Standing over the crowd of seated reporters, I was now able to spot my father, although I never would have recognized him if he weren't sitting next to Isabelle.

"Who is it upsetting my courtroom?"

Richard tugged at my dress. "Elsie, sit down."

"I am Elsie Lutz." I jumped down and stomped my way toward the front. "And that man there is my father."

A bailiff sitting near the gate that separated the spectators from the main courtroom held me back from advancing farther.

"Sweet child, I am going to have to ask you to leave the courtroom for your behavior."

I couldn't back down, not with Grin in the hospital, my frail father sitting two steps from me, and Isabelle sacrificing her honor to help him. I stood my ground.

"Tell me, sir," I said, "why is it that newsboys who have no money, very little shelter, and no food took a girl like me into their brotherhood as one of their own, but you, sir, who have money, plenty of shelter, and food on your table, do not do the same?" The courtroom went silent. "I have been with boys who had nothing and spoke for what they believed in. And they helped me, you see, because they showed me that I was much more than a quiet little girl, that I had a voice, and there are some voices that need to be heard. Miss Thornton is one of those voices, sir, and you should let her speak. So I am telling you now, I want her to be my father's lawyer."

The room was quiet while everyone held their breath.

"I could have you thrown in jail for contempt of court, little missy."

I swallowed hard, not regretting having spoken. "If that's your decision, that is your right as the judge. My father should also have the right to the counsel of his choosing."

The judge looked down at his papers. Isabelle looked at me with tears in her eyes.

Mr. Smith, the prosecutor, stood. "The state in no way finds Miss Thornton's representing Mr. Lutz an issue, Your Honor. Be that your decision," he finished condescendingly.

"Child, take a seat," the judge motioned.

"Sir…" I began to protest again.

"Take a seat, young lady," he stated clearly, his eyebrows raised in my direction. "*Proceed* with your case, Miss Thornton."

The reporters erupted in applause, and my heart leapt. Even my father managed a smile. The judge banged his gavel a few more times amid the cheers, and Isabelle waited a moment for it to die down before proceeding.

"This man, Dietrich Lutz, has suffered weeks in prison for a crime he didn't commit, for a crime he wasn't even there to commit. Let's not have him waste any more time away from his daughter."

The prosecution's main witness was the man with the accusatory finger from the railroad tracks the day my father was arrested.

He climbed onto the stand and was so nervous he didn't even look up from his feet. Mr. Smith stood to question him.

"You were there the night that John Pyle was shot, is that correct?"

"Yes 'ir."

"And you saw the man who shot John Pyle."

"Yes 'ir."

"And who was it?"

"That man there, from what I can remember."

"From what you can remember?"

"There were quite a few men there that night that worked for the surface railroad. I remember remarking about the tall German man. When Johnny was shot, I started asking around. One of the guys said there was a tall German man that worked over on Fortieth and Vanderbilt. I went to see and that looked just like the man, just like 'im."

Mr. Smith was pleased by this answer. "No further questions."

The judge turned his gaze to Isabelle.

Isabelle smoothed out her dress as she walked to the stand to cross-examine the man.

"There are many tall German men in the city, aren't there?"

"Yes 'um."

"So how are you so sure that it was this man that you saw?"

"Well, it looks like 'im. Plus he worked at the railroad, the only people there at the Trolley Strike were those that worked for the railroad."

"For the surface railroad."

He faltered, "Yes."

"But Mr. Lutz doesn't work for the surface railroad."

The man's face went pale. "But I was sure it was him. Lots of men who worked for the trolley went to then work at Vanderbilt and Fortieth."

"And the other way around?"

"Huh?"

"Men who worked at Vanderbilt went and striked for the trolley workers?"

The reporters laughed at this absurdity.

"Well, I…" the man stumbled.

"Would you say a man who had worked at Vanderbilt for the last two years would be motivated to strike in Brooklyn for the trolley workers?"

The man shook his head no.

"I wouldn't think so either."

Isabelle nodded in conclusion and took a seat, appearing satisfied with the answer.

I myself wanted to get up and say a few things, but knowing it would only hinder Isabelle's case, I stayed put.

For his next witness, Mr. Smith called the deputy chief to the stand. I was asked to leave the courtroom since the details of the murder were not appropriate for a child. I did not protest and left with Richard. Outside the courtroom, he bought me ice cream from a peddler. It wasn't a hokey-pokey cart, but it was still very good.

By the time we returned, the prosecution had finished with its witnesses and Mrs. Krol was ascending the stand.

"Mrs. Krol? Isabelle got Mrs. Krol to testify?" I remarked in awe to Richard.

"Yes," Richard nodded. "She's a stubborn one."

"I know."

Isabelle began, "Mrs. Anka Krol, you know Dietrich well?"

"Ya, he and his daughter have boarded with me for two years. That was until both of them mysteriously disappeared a couple weeks ago leaving me without boarders and bills to pay. But that is a separate matter," she concluded in her Polish accent.

"And their disappearance was after the arrest on July fifteenth?"

"Yes, it was July fifteenth."

"Now, do you remember the night before July fifteenth?"

"My son had been very ill. That night he had a fever."

"Objection," shot up Mr. Smith. "Are we to believe that this woman can really recall any night off the top of her head?"

Isabelle interrupted, "Please let the witness explain."

"Objection overruled," mumbled the judge.

Mr. Smith, uneasy about where this was going, straightened his vest and took a seat back down.

"Mrs. Krol, why do you remember this night?"

"It was the anniversary of my husband's death."

The crowd "awwed" in respect. Mr. Smith looked greatly unhappy.

"And you can relate to Dietrich Lutz in this respect?"

"Ya, he lost his wife too."

"You said that night your son had a fever?"

"Ya."

"Objection," Mr. Smith interrupted. "Is this relevant?"

"Overruled," the judge smirked. "Mr. Smith, take a seat, and let the woman continue."

"I asked young Elsie to take my son in her bed with her so that I might have one peaceful night of sleep. I don't blame the girl for turning me down. My son is a restless sleeper."

"So restless," Isabelle added, "that he kept you up all night?"

"Ya, I kept a pot on and would help him with some steam every hour or so."

"The point of this, Your Honor?" snapped Mr. Smith.

"The point," Isabelle continued, sauntering from the witness stand to the jury box, "is that you would be an expert witness as to whether Mr. Lutz left your home at all that night."

"Ya, and he didn't."

The reporters mumbled to one another with fervor.

"Can you be sure?"

"Ya, he never left."

I smiled at Richard. "I could have told them that," I whispered.

Mrs. Krol exited the stand, and Isabelle took the floor for her final words. She paced about the men, confident and assured.

"Gentlemen of the jury, because this man could not defend himself, he has been ridiculed and placed under false arrest. All they have is one man's account, which directly contradicts the account of Mrs. Anka Krol. It is a shame what happened to Mr. Pyle, and it's a shame that you must choose between the testimonies of a man and that of a woman. But you must remember the facts: that Mr. Lutz did not work for the surface railroad and was not affiliated with the strike in any way. He is a father whose only responsibility was to take care of his daughter, who then was homeless on the street because of his mistaken identity. I pray that you rectify this mistake now and rule in favor of the innocent father Dietrich Lutz."

I wasn't allowed to approach my father during the minutes that elapsed between Isabelle's final words and the announcement that the jury had reached a verdict. These moments were truly torture. My fate was in the hands of twelve men who had been led away to a room to discuss my father's innocence or guilt.

During this time, all I could do was focus on my broken, ratty old black boots.

Even in their frail state, the material that formed the boots had been strong enough to continue to carry me day after day until this point. My mother's words that these shoes would grant me equality never rang so true as in that moment. It wasn't until these shoes were in their most frail and broken state that they took me through some of the greatest lessons of my life. These black boots were me, with their laces wrapping the soles to their frame, rigged to get through one more day. I would never have come so far if I hadn't first been broken.

"We have a verdict," Richard whispered, running to my side after speaking with Isabelle.

I took a deep breath.

"Whatever happens," Richard explained, "I want you to know that Isabelle, William, and I are here to take care of you, no matter what Aunt Sophie tries to do with you. Even if that means one of us becomes your legal guardian."

Richard's gesture was so tender, and at any other moment the thought would have put a smile on my face, but any world without my father seemed like a very cold and dark place that I didn't want to think about. Not even for one minute.

"And how do you find the defendant?" Judge Quigley's voice rang through the silenced courtroom.

The lead juror stood, a piece of paper outstretched in his hand. The men beside him were stone-cold in their expressions.

"We find Dietrich Lutz, in the murder of John Pyle, not guilty."

I threw up my hands in victory and ran as fast as I could up the courtroom aisle toward my father. His thin body nearly crumbled under my weight. He embraced me with his arms, and I never wanted to leave. Isabelle nearly fell over as she joined us in our embrace. Finally, I thought, finally it was over.

Chapter XVIII

The Journal

Isabelle's father was waiting for us when we returned. As I stood next to my pa, with my hand in his, it warmed my heart even further to see Mr. Thornton embrace his daughter with love and acceptance. Ironically, Isabelle's dramatic entrance onto the New York scene defending and exonerating an immigrant superseded any false scandal that was plaguing Mr. Thornton, and his name soon dropped from the papers.

After the trial, Isabelle helped us find an apartment far from the gloom of Orchard Street in the mid-twenties on the west side of Manhattan. It was a lovely building and not far from Papa's new job as a grocery store clerk at the local German market. What I loved the most was the park nearby. It was one of the few parks in the city built by Reformers to keep children from playing in the street. It had a single oak tree that offered shade from the burning sun. It even housed a few birds that could be heard in the early morning.

As far as the other newsboys, it was only two days after the incident in the tunnel that Hearst and Pulitzer passed through their circulation managers, and not the union, that they would keep the price at sixty cents a ten, but the boys could return all papers they didn't sell for a hundred percent refund. The union refused again, but the newsboys—they're their own businessmen just like Grin had said—felt it was fair, compromised, and went back to work, rejoicing in a victory.

The gangs went about their normal everyday routines, and eventually the union diminished. I saw the Vincent boys only one time after that fateful summer. The Newsboy Home had organized a Christmas dinner to celebrate the "summer we licked them." I attended and enjoyed seeing the boys again. Kid was back leading the pack, in the good graces of all the Vincents. The belief that he had betrayed them was quickly erased from the boys' memories. In fact, many of the newsboys' versions of what happened that summer were greatly exaggerated. Although the brotherhood was lively as always, it wasn't the same without Grin. It only made me miss him more.

Papa was working his day shift the Saturday I decided to finally read Grin's journal. The green leaves of summer were starting to turn to a reddish sheen, and the fall breeze was whipping through the streets, shaking the branches of the oak tree. I had saved his diary, hidden in my possessions, to savor when life was quiet, like a prized red hot from Mitchell's, too valuable to consume quickly.

I cracked open the pages and sifted through them tenderly, like I was trespassing in Grin's private thoughts.

Returning to the first page, I saw big black letters traced over a million times in pencil:

This here is Grin's. If ya are reading these words, ya better stop or ya will be soaked.

The next page began with new penmanship, soft small letters scrunched up on the page, barely legible. I brought the journal in closer to make out the words.

The rain is pourin down on this church roof above. I hate the winter in New York. It's lousy for sellin papes. It's even more lousy that I have no one for Christmas. Found this journal wrapped and abandoned on 34th in the Macy's alley, my Christmas gift. Never had anythin special like this come my way before, so I'm aimin to make the most of it.

I read on to discover that Grin had amazing stories from his days on the street, some of courage and bravery, others comical. But after a few months, Grin stopped writing. A couple pages following the last story had some random drawings, a map of Grin's favorite routes, and some scribbled math adding up the money from the year. And then, after pages of nonsense and doodles, Grin started writing again.

Made a pretty little girl trip today. She has the most beautiful eyes I've even seen, like the sun shines in them. She was workin with her pa at Vanderbilt. When I came back an hour later, I noticed the same girl and her pa in some trouble. Then, the last thing I expect, she was runnin after the police wagon shoutin for him. She couldn't keep goin and lost where the wagon went, so I took off on the rooftops to see if I could follow it. I lost it too. Next thing, the little girl was gone. I wonder what her pa did...

My heart lept, remembering that day, realizing that he thought I was pretty. He never told me that.

She shouldn't be a newsboy. I can't let her near the Vincents. They could drag her into the strike. She could get killed! I want to take her to Annie's, but I think I'll scare her off if I mention it...

I was surprised that Grin appeared to have a plan. Whoever Annie was, it was another one of his many contacts Mikey must have been going on about. I felt foolish for doubting him. He was right: joining the strike did put my life in danger, and for the first time, I realized that he suffered for it.

Met William Randolph Hearst. Yeah, Hearst! But he's not gonna respect the boys. They'll need to get the big newspaper ad men involved, and a newsboy can't be president of the union. He's not gonna listen. I must convince Kid.

I closed the tender leather covers. Somehow having it near me made it feel like Grin never left. I went years without realizing that that feeling was more than one of friendship. With him gone, I would never fully know what those feelings meant until I was much older and hindsight would tell me that it was love.

I thought about him all the time and how my life would have been if I hadn't met him. Whenever I thought about those days, I smiled. And then I would think of Grin in his new life. I imagined him on the farm, fresh from plowing the field, curled up under a tree and writing in a new journal.

My mother was right: I did have a strong voice. But it had been deep inside me. It was a new voice that had resurrected it, strengthened it and called it forth. A voice that was never my own, but was that of a newsboy with a wide sly grin.

EPILOGUE

Reunion

You are cordially invited to the
10th Annual Isabelle Thornton Scholarships Luncheon
On Saturday May 3rd, 1969
At the Tavern on the Green,
Central Park, New York City, New York

~

Keynote address by Elsie Lutz Walden

Once the quaint brick sheepfold that housed the herd of Central Park's Sheep Meadow, Tavern on the Green had been resurrected as a prime New York City restaurant. I had always loved dining there ever since my husband and I celebrated our thirtieth wedding anniversary in the Elm Tree Room.

Because Sheep Meadow was where I first met Isabelle, I insisted the foundation choose it as the annual location for the luncheon to honor the recipients of the college scholarships. The outside garden was perfect for the event, peppered with tables surrounded by red and green chairs tucked under the shady American elms.

The five young female guests of honor and their families settled in, and I tenderly made my way to the front table. Walking was getting harder these days, which is to be expected at eighty-three years of age.

"May I have your attention," commanded Susan, the chairwoman.

The room settled.

"I'm honored today to introduce not only the woman responsible for the establishment of the Isabelle Thornton Foundation, but a noted woman of influence in her own right for her tireless work for woman suffrage and labor laws in the early part of this century. Please help me welcome our keynote speaker and founder of the foundation, Mrs. Elsie Lutz Walden."

The crowd applauded, and I took my usual place at the center table overlooking the fifty guests.

"Well, now, thank you," I began. "It is always an honor to come and see the faces of young women beginning their careers with help from the foundation. In many ways, I was the first woman to benefit from Isabelle Thornton's generosity. She guided me through my days in college and was the one who introduced me to the National American Woman Suffrage Association.

"In fact," I continued, "I met Isabelle seventy years ago, right over there."

I pointed to my left, to Sheep Meadow, surrounded by the lush green trees of Central Park. It had not housed the wayward sheep since the Depression in the 1930s, when honorable New Yorkers feared for the lives of the flock. The park agreed the sheep were too tempting a prize for hungry vagabonds, and the herd was quickly removed to Brooklyn.

Looking at that meadow always reminded me of Isabelle. And being reminded of Isabelle always brought me right back to that summer of 1899 and the memory of another fateful influence on my life.

"The next years may make little mark on your careers," I continued, "but they will be a time you cherish in your heart because they will make you who you are as you strive for your dreams."

I took a deep breath. My words to the young girls were truer than they knew. I had years of documented accomplishments, a marriage to kind man who impacted the country in his own right as a politician, and four strapping sons who forged their own paths in the world. The year my husband became sick and passed away, I had shared with him my story about the newsboys. He quickly fixated on the coincidental encounter with Isabelle, as most people did, and tossed aside the details that got me there. No one could ever understand how special that lone newsboy was to me, and I figured no one ever would.

I continued my address. "Many people feel like they know everything about someone because they've read history books with their name in them. However, what makes someone who they are, are not the documented details and accomplishments, but what happened in between. These are the special moments of our hearts that we share with no one because they are too precious to be recorded."

Reaching down to the table, I grabbed the book I had carried with me when I spoke before juries, before the NAWSA National Convention, even before the Senate of the United States. Flipping open the worn leather-bound cover, I read the passage I had added to the last page of the book. There was no need for my glasses—I had read it so many times that it was burned into my memory.

"I would like to share a quote from the writer George Eliot: 'The golden moments in the stream of life rush past us, and we see nothing but sand. The angels come to visit us, and we only know them when they are gone. How shall we live so as at the end to have done the most for others and make the most of ourselves?'"

I closed the book tenderly and put it down by my side.

"My hope is that you do the most for others and make the most of yourselves," I concluded, seeing many of the girls' eyes glazing over. "Well now... Let's begin, shall we?"

Susan stood and handed over the list of names.

"If you could please stand when your named is called, we would love to honor you with applause." I cleared my throat. "Janet Richey ... Caroline Tihen ... Judith Charles ... Edith Franklin ... and Annabelle—" I stopped cold, nearly stumbling over the name before me. I checked it again, and then at the risk of fainting sputtered out "Annabelle Grinnan?"

I looked up from the paper to the table where the beaming young girl stood, her family applauding in support. On the far right corner, his eyes fixed on mine, was an old man in a brown suit with a calm smile.

"Excuse me," I said, nearly collapsing in my seat.

Susan came to my side. "Are you all right?

"Yes, yes ... fine."

"Um ..." Susan gathered her thoughts. "Let's partake in this lovely lunch; then we will proceed with the honors."

The crowd clapped in conclusion and turned their chairs back to their tables. I, however, was unable to take my eyes off the old man.

I tried to act calm as the guests finished their meals, my mind swirling with the possibility, the hope, that this would be the reunion I had always hoped for.

Susan concluded the luncheon with a fine speech, honoring the ladies and their accomplishments. By the end, knots were twisting in my stomach. I didn't know what I would say. Finally, with closing applause, the guests rose from their seats and milled around shaking hands and congratulating one another.

I couldn't wait any longer and stood. With weak legs, I proceeded to the table of the Grinnan family. Immediately sensing my presence, the young eighteen-year-old Annabelle spun around.

"Mrs. Walden! It is such a pleasure to meet you," beamed Annabelle as she stood. "I did a report about you in tenth grade."

"Thank you. Congratulations." I smiled, looking around the table. It was filled with Annabelle's younger brother. Next to him was their mother, a spitting image of Annabelle, and their father, tall with blond hair and a slight resemblance to the older man next to him. My eyes settled on the man in the brown suit, his face tucked under an eight-panel cap often associated with newsboys.

"Thank you!" she said. Then realizing she might have lettuce in her teeth, she quickly closed her mouth, never losing her smile. "Oh! Please let me introduce my mother, Grace, and father, Michael, and my grandfather, Henry."

The old man stood and stepped forward. My heart plummeted to my stomach.

"Henry ... so it is you." I smiled, tears in my eyes.

Annabelle's smile dropped to shock. "You know each other?"

At his smile broadened, he slipped back into the young boy I once knew. I could no longer hold back my tears.

"This is the boy who changed my life."

"Elsie," he whispered, coming near to me.

We embraced. My fragile arms could barely grip fully around his torso.

"What? Grandpa?" exclaimed the young girl. "But you read my report on her ... You never said anything ..."

"Some things are too precious to be shared," he said, echoing my earlier speech.

"Wait, is this how I got the scholarship?"

Grin laughed. "No. Elsie and I haven't spoken since I was fifteen years old."

Annabelle's father stood, "Dad, is this ...?"

Grin nodded.

Annabelle watched in confusion as Grin took my hand and led me across the Central Park loop onto a familiar neighboring park bench overlooking Sheep Meadow.

"I never heard from you," I muttered, still shaking my head, still in disbelief.

"You were living your dream, and I was living mine," he merely whispered.

I took his hand, wrinkled and worn. It was a perfect match to mine.

"What is that?" he asked, pointing to the small journal in my hands. I looked down, having completely forgotten that it was in my possession. I passed it to him.

"My journal?" he remarked with surprise. "You kept it all these years?"

"It was a little piece of you, and a little piece of me."

He caressed its binding.

"I loved what happened with the cow in Brooklyn." I laughed, recalling the stories I had read many times.

"On Flatbush ..." he remembered.

"I visited them."

"Ya did?"

"I helped them years later in a lawsuit."

Grin took a deep breath and smiled. We sat in peaceful harmony. I felt thirteen once again, and I was sure he felt fifteen. I had lived with his stories from his journal for many years and had wondered about the man who had become of them. I felt in that moment I did know, and he knew me.

Grin caressed my hand. I closed my eyes at his touch. Not much needed to be said. Somewhere underneath this great city rumbled the subway trains making their way to Grand Central Station, where it all began. And although the two of us on that park bench may have looked like the end, it didn't feel that way. In fact, by finding ourselves together again, we realized we were with each other all along.

Historical Note

The newsboy strike began on July 20, 1899 and lasted until August 2, when William Randolph Hearst of the *New York World* and Joseph Pulitzer of the *New York Journal* compromised with the newsboys, giving them "return rights," that is, allowing them to sell back their papers at one-hundred percent.

The names of all the newsboys mentioned in this book were recorded in New York's other newspapers in 1899: the *Tribune*, the *Sun*, the *Times*, and the *Brooklyn Eagle*, who were more than happy to write about the circulation loss suffered by their rivals. These papers give a colorful portrayal of the newsboys and their fight. Here I have given a fictional portrayal of real events, such as the meeting at Irving Hall, the fights and arrests of the boys who "soaked" scabs, and the betrayal of Kid Blink and Dave Simmons.

Although Elsie is fictional, she is based on many young immigrant women who existed in New York at the time. Isabelle Thornton is also based on real women at the turn of the century who became the first female lawyers of their day, and subsequently, the driving force behind the suffrage movement that lead to the 19th Amendment: women's right to vote.

For more information about the real life events and people that inspired this book visit http://callingextra.com

Selected Bibliography

Brooklyn Eagle, July 20, 21, 24, 26, 30, 1899.

Drachman, Virginia. *Sisters in Law*. Cambridge: Harvard University Press, 1998.

Dulberger, Judith. *Mother Donit Fore the Best*. Syracuse: Syracuse University Press, 1996.

Gunckel, John. *Boyville*. Toledo: The Franklin Company, 1905

Leslie, Madeline. *Never Give Up; or The News-Boys (The Leslie Stories)*. Boston: Graves & Young, 1863.

Morrow, Johnny. *A Voice of the Newsboys*. New York: Barnes & Burr, 1860

Nasaw, David. *Children of the City At Work and At Play*. New York: Oxford University Press, 1985

New York Times, July 21-31 and August 1 1899.

New York Sun, July 20-29, 31 and August 1-2 1899.

New York Tribune, July 21-31 and August 1-2, 1899.

Wertheimer, Barbara. *We were there : the story of working women in America.* New York: Pantheon Books, 1977.

About the Author

Kristina Romero began her career as an actress on CBS Daytime's *As the World Turns,* where she earned Daytime Emmy nominations for Outstanding Younger Actress in 2001 and 2002.

Having earned her Master's in Professional Writing from the University of Southern California, Kristina has written and directed numerous projects. Currently, she lives outside Washington, DC with her husband and son.

CPSIA information can be obtained
at www.ICGtesting.com
Printed in the USA
LVHW032113060622
720620LV00001B/176